This is a work of fiction. All the characters and events portrayed in this book are fictional, and any resemblance to real people or actions is purely coincidental.

Turtle Bay

A Shamus Pickford Story

By

David Earth

David Earth's other titles:

A Trip to the Myakka Cutoff
By-Catch
The Riviera Marina!

Author's Note:

The Shamus Pickford stories are all rooted in Southwest Florida where I aim to inject culture, the working man/woman struggles, the hardships, and the underbellies of everyday Floridians into my work. At times, I feel I've done them justice.

Florida's rapid growth has made it increasingly difficult for the simple-living waterman to sustain his way of life. That's one of the reasons I felt compelled to write these stories—to preserve in amber the "way it was," as vital to our cultural memory as plankton is to an oyster. With so much of Florida's past being swallowed up and paved over, the responsibility of remembering what once was now falls to longtime locals and storytellers.

These stories were written in the quiet hours—on days off, in stolen moments of spare time. The locations described throughout these books, and in most of my salt-soaked work, are real places, or at least, they were when the stories first took shape. As I write this, some of those very spots stand on the brink of erasure, threatened by the steady march of development. Bearing witness to this transformation provides a constant, if bittersweet, source of inspiration.

Year after year people flock to Florida, in specifics the Southwest coast, where it's dodged the dozers longer than the east coast. But as of late, it seems Pandora's box has finally been open. Huge corporations have, over time, weaseled their way into the community, funded many different programs to the unwitting recipients, only to come collect in the way of environmental destruction.

This note is by no means a call to protest. Growth is a force that cannot be stopped but must be done with the environment a top concern.

The short Shamus Pickford books can be on the technical side, some confusing lingo, or mentions of a strange location, that may only be familiar to the locals, who have lived in the areas described. It was not intentionally written that way.

Getting these stories "out there" has been an arduous process with many setbacks. It's hard to say whether I'd continue these past three or four.

The first blip of Shamus Pickford and his associates came to me when a friend and I were casting lures at a dock in a private basin on the east coast of Charlotte Harbor in the early 2000s (nearly 20 years before its first publication). I came to understand it from the bow of my skiff, watching the land flatten beneath the teeth of machines, as hulking new structures rose faster than the eye could blink. The basin described in these pages is real—still there, still fished, still breathing—but like so much of old Florida, its days may be numbered. The model for Shamus's house with the boat ramp was there at one point, only to have been torn down, and in its place a monstrosity of a house built overtop the ruins. Growth is growth.

It was sad to see it go, and I tried to remember it the best I could. I'd spent a lot of time fishing in that basin and along those docks, that I felt the need to preserve its memory, or at least a vague motif.

These books are not perfect. They aren't massive works of literature either, but I hope they capture interest, if only for a moment. When it was time to sit down and finally hash these things out, I did a good portion out on my skiff. The rough drafts lived nomadically in my head for years and prying them out clearly, and onto paper, was no easy task.

They were written mostly outdoors, which is where I choose to write the majority of my stories—it's where the muse is the strongest. Outdoors can be extremely inspirational. For me, a fine view and a cup of coffee is motivation at its best. I've had an on-again off-again relationship with this series over many years before struggling to their final drafts. I honestly thought I'd never finish them, but here we are.

"I'm so happy because today I found my
friends—they're in my head."
--Kurt Cobain

"Maybe everyone is too rich. I have noticed that
there is no dissatisfaction like that of the rich.
Feed a man, clothe him, put him in a good
house, and he will die of despair."
--Lee, the Cantonese cook (EOE)

"Shallow up, man. (It meant stop being serious;
leave the burdens of depth behind.)"
--Tomlinson (RWW)

"I see myself as just doomed, pitiful—An awful
realization that I have been fooling myself all my
life thinking there was a next thing to do to keep
the show going and actually I'm just a sick clown
and so is everyone else."
--Jack Kerouac (Big Sur)

Turtle Bay

Prologue

Drawn by the promise of a warm winter refuge along the Southwest Florida coast, it was nothing unusual, for much of the year, to see an unfamiliar man wandering the aisles of Frank's, the local tackle shop in Port Charlotte.

Behind the counter, a clerk flipping through the latest issue of *WaterLife* magazine glanced up and offered a nod to the stranger—an easy, practiced gesture he gave to customers hundreds of times a day.

The unfamiliar man nodded back, slinked to a waist-high chest freezer to appear interested, removed a frozen mullet, and tapped it on the freezer's lid.

Above the freezer, a corkboard held tacked, overlapped Polaroids. In them, people were presenting various species of fish, from snook to redfish to king mackerel. He swept across the photos and strolled the aisles, frowning at the lingering fishermen, where not one person fit the position's needs. He wanted a man who had in-depth knowledge of Charlotte Harbor—a commercial fisherman, a charter fishing guide perhaps— to aid him in navigating though the shallow waters of Turtle Bay. He'd heard through word of mouth that if he couldn't find such a man at Frank's then they didn't exist.

After returning the mullet, the man advanced to a wall hanging soft-plastic lures. He picked out a bag of glitter-doused baits, squinted to read the lettering. The door's entrance chime sounded and in walked a tall, broad-shouldered man.

The clerk, who dropped the magazine atop the glass counter, raised his chin upward. "Eliot, how are you?"

"I'm good, good."

The clerk tongue-swiped the toothpick to the opposite corner of his mouth. "Keeping your line wet, I hope?"

"Sure am—yup." Eliot Waldrup's thumbs were looped through his front two belt holes. He surfed through the assortment of reels showcased under the display counter's glass.

When the unfamiliar man from the aisle heard the name Eliot, his attention left the bag of glinting baits and focused on the counter. "There he is," he whispered.

1

My old friend Klinger Lee Nowell blared country rock through his open truck window as he motored up my driveway.

It was rare these days that I had time to take personal fishing trips. I'd spent all of spring catering to my charter fishing clientele, using their hard-earned money to create a take-home experience, one that might award them bragging rights among their work constituents. Delivering a cozy sensation that their money had been well-spent catching a trophy fish … is what I do.

Charter fishing is a competitive business, a time-gobbling profession that, by the end of tarpon season, leaves a man dog tired. I do it illegitimately, which means no license and no rules. If a client asked why my prices were so low, I freely explain my lack of a Captain's license, and my reasoning behind it. Nobody had ever refused because of it.

I stood in the dark under the garage door facing the driveway.

Klinger's truck, an old rusted-out Chevy 1500, rattled as it came to a squeaky stop. Chipped paint surrounded the door handles and a rotted tailgate hung from a shard of rusted hinge.

Klinger's head turned, and squinting one eye shut, tossed me the right kind of smile—one that meant even though he'd arrived with a significant hangover, good times were coming our way.

His arm rested along the window jamb, a store-bought foam cup of coffee cradled in his hand. "Mornin', Shamus."

If I had to guess, an intense night of overindulgence resulted in his rough appearance. His voice, when he wasn't hungover, resembled a two-stroke weed eater, but today it seemed a bit hoarse, like someone who'd consumed a whole pack of smokes.

Klinger partied harder than a country boy winning a fishing tournament, so seeing him heavy-footed this morning was quite a sight. On normal fishing mornings, a wired-up, animated Klinger spoke a million words an hour. But not today. His wiry frame dropped sluggishly from the truck, foam cup held by his teeth, had a bag of ice in one hand, and a twelve-pack of beer tucked under the other. Along with a fresh sunburn, his floppy blond hair sprouted from a red visor. A pair of khaki cargo shorts drooped below his waist, weighed down by the contents of his pockets. A tight, blue tank top wrapped his torso and his keys jangled while he walked.

"Rough night?" I asked.

"Got tarp'n blood, man." To have tarpon blood was my friend's way of declaring his seaworthiness.

"Did you grab food?" I asked.

"Yup, got righ'ere." He reached onto the Chevy's splitting leather passenger seat where it had been scratched open to the yellow foam. He pulled out another bag holding sunflower seeds.

I said, "Cooler's in the boat."

Klinger, a fifth-generation Florida native—or otherwise known as a Gator—received the tag "Klinger" during his raucous, unhinged days as a toddler. At first, giving him a proper-fitting name baffled his parents, then his observant grandfather one day asked, "Why he always clingin' on Mama's leg like some koala bear clingin' to a tree?" From that day forward, the whole family called him Klinger—he kept the name.

Klinger dropped the beer in the cooler and snagged a tangle of rods and tackle from the bed of his truck.

Last week, I'd traded a twenty-five-foot enclosed trailer for an old Toyota pickup running at two-hundred-and-fifty thousand miles. A vehicle's mileage might as well be its age. My sun-fried brain wasn't a fan of tedious electronics that companies pack into every nook and cranny. I prefer the simple and easy. No power windows or locks? No problem—fewer things to break.

Klinger brought himself a cup, but I always offer morning guests coffee. "If you're interested, I made fresh Joe. Just have to pour it?"

Klinger lifted the cup. "Got some already. And dang, man..." he said, noticing my yard, "...ya gotta mow your grass."

"Why don't you mow it for me?" I countered. "You're the one with the lawn business."

Klinger's head swiveled. "Well, Shamus. If you'd clean up the yard a bit more, maybe I would. You a thirty-year-old man, and 'ave a lawn like this? I ain't riskin' damagin' m'equipment runnin' over God knows what's hidin' out under all this overgrowin' nonsense."

I smiled. "Nice one."

The tall grass might pose an issue for some, but not me. My house rests on three-and-a-half acres of overgrown palmettos, unmanicured sable palms, invasive Brazilian pepper trees, and irritating patches of desert-like sugar sand. I haven't clipped the lawn in two summers. One-and-a-half acres sits in the frontside, and two acres spreads on the backside, leading to the canal, where I have a single-wide boat ramp.

I climbed behind the wheel of my truck, and after positioning it for launch, I waited in the cab while Klinger walked ahead of the skiff to assist in the trailer hitch alignment.

"Keep it comin'," he said, red-faced from the brake lights.

Klinger held his hands out for me, inching them together, which displayed an exact measurement between the trailer hitch and the coupler.

"Here we go. Slow now … okay, okay. Nice 'en easy … 'ats it!" He raised a closed fist, the international sign for stop.

Once we finished attaching the trailer to the truck, I went into the house. Before heading back to the garage, I glanced across the un-mowed yard and remembered the stray pup—the golden-brown cur mix that had, for now, claimed my near-empty neighborhood as home, so being an animal lover I usually leave out a full bowl of dry dog food.

The last time I spotted the pup, it appeared skinny, skin stretched tight across the ribcage, exposing outlines of thin bone; legs knobby, a bit of tail mange, but nothing that proper care couldn't trounce. My best guess put the brown-spotted female at a year old. After multiple attempts to befriend the animal, most mornings she'd snatched the food and ran. I wouldn't damn-near see her at all most days, just a tipped over, licked-clean bowl.

In the garage, Klinger was rotating my homemade rod carousel, inspecting a plethora of my finest fishing rods. "What yah bringin' t'day?"

"Same as always, I guess." I sipped my coffee, chewing over choices of gear as well, weighing out various fish-catching scenarios in my head, combining different sized reels with different sized rods, all having a specific purpose. I decided to bring a tarpon rig for the likelihood we'd smack into a school willing to bite. Being early July, we had a high probability of crossing paths with the mighty Silver King. If I'd crossed paths with a tarpon while on charter and had no gear to offer, I'd feel the client's disappointment straight through the monetary tip, but with Klinger, the pressure was off.

I also snagged a Penn Battle 4000 series fishing reel with fifteen-pound Power Pro line strapped on a 7'6" medium-light Redbone. A Stradic 3000, my principal lure reel, wound full in ten-pound braided line, rounded out the trifecta.

I rolled the rear garage door up high and tight. My RV-sized garage sat just a hundred feet from where the boat ramp sloped into the water. With both the front and back roll-up doors perfectly aligned, I could back the trailer straight through the garage and down into the bay without ever needing to turn.

Attached to the truck at the base of the boat ramp, I hopped into the boat and waited to be launched. A boat ramp behind the house was an advantage without which I couldn't live. Using my truck, Klinger reversed the trailer down the ramp while I sat at the helm.

"Wait!" I called. "Stop!"

"Wha'in the——?" Klinger said through the rear sliding window.

"Let me check the plug," I shouted, descending from the boat and ducking under the stern. Not once had I ever forgotten to tighten the plug, but over the years, I'd seen too many close calls. Even the most seasoned boaters could spiral into panic when their twenty-thousand-dollar rig started to sink—all because of a forgotten drain plug. So, my pre-launch ritual was necessary.

I showed Klinger a thumbs-up while boarding the boat. "Okay, go ahead, slow now."

Klinger reversed an additional twenty-five feet before hitting the brakes again. The light skiff slipped off the trailer, lying on a bed of glass-flat water.

Ten years ago, I wished to elevate my charter fishing business to the next level, so obviously I needed a new skiff. Equipped with a wide beam and shallow transom, and a gunwale measuring ten inches above the water, it was spacious enough to fish three people in reasonable comfort.

She began firing after I turned the key. The scent of two-stroke oil mixing with fuel and combusting inside a mathematically precise chamber, then exhausting into the air, for me, was the proper aromatic pleasure first thing in the morning. Some people prefer coffee, but not me.

After a glance at the house, I thought of how luck had found me, that I owned my own home, and with it, a boat ramp that opened into a mammoth, oyster-laden, saltwater basin that contained, and sheltered, the precious mangrove shrub. My nearest neighbor lived clear-out of shouting range.

A few years back, Hurricane Charley's unwelcome hand nearly destroyed it, leaving demolition as its likely fate. The previous owners had abandoned it, and after many months of patience, I scooped it up for the same price as a five-hundred-pound tuna.

After sliding the sixty horsepower in gear, idling fifteen feet to the dock, I waited for Klinger, scanning the water surface, looking for any undulations that indicated a dolphin's presence.

Klinger lumbered to the dock, flip-flops smacking the backs of his feet. He eased across the plank, over a sea grape limb, paused, and inched down.

"Careful, don't fall," I said.

"Yah need t'fix this, man."

Over the years, I'd made countless half-hearted attempts to repair the wobbly dock, none of them worth much more than wishful thinking. It measured an exact twenty feet by ten feet, and just one cleat was structurally stable. Even with its missing pine floorboards and rotted-out floor joist, it still kept the skiff safe during storms.

Parts of the seawall were damaged too, exposing rebar, and in pathetic fashion, chipped-off concrete chunks crumbled into the water. Using a twenty-foot plank, I bridged fifteen feet of treacherous gap, securing it from a solid point on the seawall to the edge of the dock. Next to the plank, a large sea grape tree overflowed onto the dock and dangled into the water.

My friend lumbered his stick-like frame into the skiff, sending out a small ripple of water. He untied a loose bowline from the cleat, sat on the bench cushion ahead of the center console, and let loose a braying yawn. "Water looks good."

A slight bubble ahead and the resident dolphin surfaced, exhaling a *pooooeeesh* into the calmness of the basin's ironed flatness. Two years ago, after Charlotte harbor emerged victorious from a hard-fought struggle against a ruinous red tide bloom, the dolphin took up permanent residence. Every morning since, it has tormented the schools of mullet that also call the basin home, before it vanishes out to the harbor to broaden its feeding grounds—or perhaps to find companionship.

Who knew for sure? But it always returns by dusk. I've been calling it Spinner.

Klinger noticed the mammal. "Remember yah dared m'ass to identify the sex of 'at dang thing?"

"You bet I do."

True story. Acting from within, Klinger's exploration-minded brain allowed his body to leap off the seawall and swim after it.

"I remember that big thing would have no part of your shenanigans and hammered you in the chest with its bottle-shaped nose…"

"Yeah … me too." He massaged a rib. "'At hurt, man. Still got a sore spot."

Off starboard, five hundred feet from my dock, dwelled my salty neighbor, Flip. Built across the canal from a dainty shrub of mangrove, a razor-sharp oyster bed made passing his house a cautious affair.

As a licensed commercial fisherman, my neighbor chose mullet as his specialty. Along the edge of the seawall, he'd lashed together two five-hundred-gallon tanks, each rigged with PVC that ran out into the water, creating a saltwater flush system. Old crab pots and cast nets for mullet were scattered across his one-acre backyard. Twin black outboards lay silent beside a derelict skiff propped up on cinderblocks. He'd roped his nineteen-foot Sheffield mid-drive mullet boat to the dock, which, even from fifty feet away, projected the sweet smell of rotting fish. Flip was in his late fifties, had skin like leather, and was the saltiest guy I'd ever met.

Aboard the tied-tight Sheffield, he began using a metal rod marked full, medium, and low to measure his fuel. By the beam of a flashlight, he read the page, already suited up in yellow waders.

Mullet-man noticed us puttering by, cleared his throat, and called out in a deep, raspy voice: "Seen schools of bull reds over at Cape Haze Point yesterdee … might be a good startin' point."

Confidence brimmed from my ears that Flip would have the answer to my next question. "Bait?" I asked.

"Just 'round Cape Haze Point, to the south," he explained. "Right awn the bar. With this tide, though, might be tough. Try chummin' 'em up in deeper water first."

Cape Haze Point was perched at the southern tip of the West Wall in Charlotte Harbor, and due to its location and eco-friendly current flow, a surfeit of Florida's most attractive fish dwelled within the seagrass, under mangroves, and inside reddish-green sand holes.

"Perfect, appreciate it," I said, and meant it.

To have Flip as my neighbor brought an advantageous element to my game, one that would be hard to go without. The time-consuming task of scouting bait first thing in the morning was a tedious morning chore, a burden I didn't need.

Klinger turned his head back to me. "I love 'at guy."

We idled away from his dock and crossed the basin toward the harbor. I slid the engine's cut-off lanyard onto my wrist and cinched it tight.

"Still wearin' the ol' engine stopper, I see."

"You remember what happened…" Although Klinger wasn't with me during the accident, he'd often heard the story.

"Sure do. Your butt went flyin' into a thick clump of mangrove. Not a good move."

Klinger spoke correctly. But speaking in detail, many moons ago, at the age of twelve, a friend bypassed his maritime duty of wearing the engine cut-off lanyard on his thirteen-foot skiff, and coincidently, we lost steering when winding through a tight, unmarked canal. The engine should have stalled when the ruckus threw my friend onto the deck. After the abrupt stop, we ended thirty feet deep in mangroves. I was splintered up with a fast-approaching wrench in my shoulder. There were no major injuries, but the event woke me up, and changed the way I navigate.

On the short ride to the open harbor, scattered clumps of oyster beds revealed raided, cracked open shells. One should take caution when entering my basin due to the unseen, hull-gouging oyster beds and the absence of navigationally important channel markers.

My pulse quickened while approaching the end of the short idle. Craving to avoid cavitating the four-bladed propeller, I adjusted the jack plate and set the tabs for the best combination of lift and speed. The emptiness of exposed crab pots that lined the shallow sandbank along the channel indicated a low tide, and the familiar scent of fast-decomposing creatures was an aromatic pleasure.

"You ready?" I asked my friend.

"Hang awn." Klinger knew I was ready and checked his pockets to secure its contents. "We gonna try the Tur'le Bay fish shack, right?"

"I'd like to." I gave the throttle a test tap, directed at him.

"Alright," he said, and his hand karate-chopped forward.

With much grace, but a poor sense of timing, a lone, white-feathered egret landed onto the bow and began to inspect the empty baitwell. The skiff lifted off after one punch of the throttle; a precise trim tab adjustment settled it on plane. The egret flew off unfulfilled.

With a saturation of good intentions, I pointed the bow toward the West Wall. A memorable day was important because fishing for pleasure had become so rare. Both Klinger and I held hope high of catching that one fish willing to pull the perfect amount of drag, one that would satisfy a primordial craving to capture nature.

On the brink of exposure, the sun's pre-show lit the horizon red, with an eventual rise from the never-ending mass of silent water, it resembled an enormous, infinite silk sheet. I settled into our journey across the harbor, and my mind wandered.

To live in Southwest Florida enabled me to arrive at a distant, mollifying place, away from roads, houses, and people, just ten minutes from my basin.

These waters have been here long before Man, and they will continue to prosper here long after. Their existence was obvious, I believe, a reminder of what life was like one hundred, two hundred, even a thousand years ago. In Florida, the notion that Man had omitted such a visually succulent area to the brutalities of environmental development, remained inconceivable. The lack of usurped growth meant that fortunate souls, like myself, had an opportunity to experience ancient history in real-time. Motivation piqued. I sped on to escape the fog of sleep.

2

It wasn't until reaching Cape Haze Point that I noticed the anchored boat—an old Stamas cruiser with a broken cabin window. Painted across a white transom, the name *Itinerant* had been stenciled in blue lettering. A newer-model thirteen-foot Boston Whaler was also lashed to the boat's stern.

Two people appeared to be aboard the *Itinerant*, one of whom seemed inconspicuously pointing binoculars at us. The other, a much taller man, stood on the edge of the wheelhouse. Even at a lean, he was the taller of the two. His shoulders hulked under a large, bald head, and he had a familiar silhouette, but the distance was too great to decipher a clear description.

I stared long enough to give a fair chance for help— proper boating etiquette among licensed captains, which I wasn't, but in good human form, I offered help when needed. This fellow mariner didn't indicate a "help" wave after moments of us locking sight, so we went on.

The sun rose in peacefulness, illuminating the harbor like a drawn-up shade. Klinger and I descended on Cape Haze Point where pelicans dove their sharp beaks for breakfast. Local boaters were privy to the fact that a deep trough, or cut, ran perpendicular along this mangrove wall.

I chose to cross the shallow sandbar here, aiming to reach the bait-rich inside bar. At this tide height, the sandbar sat just six inches to a foot beneath the surface. I scanned it, searching for a spot that held adequate water for my shallow-draft skiff. Sighting half-submerged mangrove roots and exposed seagrass tops, I knew the water was shallow, a minor miscalculation, but not enough to stop us.

Klinger shouted, "What yah thinkin', Shamus?"

"Might get a bit skinny," I answered. "Hold on."

Klinger pointed hard, signaling to a small cut, no bigger than an average-sized driveway. "Righ'air, go!"

I aimed the skiff at it, but still had to cross twenty yards of shallow grass flats before arriving at the desired water depth. I hammered the throttle. The engine reached six thousand RPMs, creating an essential burst of speed. The propeller cavitated and screamed like hell when I raised the jack plate to maximum height. I eyed the gauges and lowered the trim tabs, which pressed the bow low against the water. I kept track of the water pressure gauge and readjusted the jack plate in accordance, inch by inch, regaining vital pressure. It was paramount that I avoided slicing seagrass, but slowing wasn't an option.

Skillfully, we skimmed smoothly across the narrow bar, and I eased back the throttle using robotic-like precision, surfing the skiff overtop its own wake. The engine returned to idle.

I glanced behind us, pausing in admiration at the path only a few would have the guts to attempt.

Even Klinger admired. He stood and reached his arms to the sky, pointed his toes, balled his fists, and stretched. "That was some skinny water righ'ere, man—good runnin'." He knelt and slurped up a handful of water. "Salts good. They'll be'ere."

*****

After Klinger's salty prediction, we settled in water five feet deep, more than enough for the lightweight skiff, and where the bait I craved swam below.

I climbed onto the poling platform as Klinger unsnapped the push pole from its holder and handed it to me. He then then yanked off his visor and jammed fingers into a tangled, dirty blond knot. "Wan' me mix up some chum?"

I scanned south. "Not yet, let's push beyond this mangrove point … to the sandbar. See if we can't spot-cast a few first."

I pushed the pole. The thrust sent us gliding as though on a magic carpet ride. Pelicans ahead skimmed the surface of the water, spearing beaks through greenback-induced ripples. I wondered how many juvenile pelicans had broken their necks piercing the surface using such unruly force. A quick gulp after lifting their heads the meal was swallowed.

"They divin' straight 'head … righ'off the bar."

Continuous stalking from the pelicans had pressed the bait into a tight, easy-to-catch pod, so we abandoned spot-casting after noticing the availability of the pelican-corralled greenbacks. Greenback, a name used mostly by locals, was by far the first choice in bait for fisherman this time of year.

"I see them," I said. "Go ahead and grab the cast net for me."

"Wan' me toss one?"

"I know you toss one hell of a cast net, but I need the practice."

"Truth…"

Klinger advanced off the front deck, slid past the console, and opened the starboard hatch. He peeked up. "Which one yah usin'?"

"Grab me the twelve-footer. Plug the baitwell, too."

"Got it."

I kept two cast nets aboard, always an eight-foot net for shallow flats, and a twelve-foot net primarily for water deeper than three feet.

I continued to pole us toward the pod of greenbacks and mumbled, "Flip, you were dead on reporting the bait. Let's hope you're correct with the redfish report."

When we touched on the school of greenbacks, the group of pelicans sensed our imposing presence as invasive and flew off with little resistance.

Klinger removed the twelve-foot net and set it on the front deck. I swiveled eastward, spotted a meal-scoping osprey. Up at two hundred feet, it had found one. I pointed to the open water.

"Hey, check that out."

Klinger was already on it. "He 'ungry for somepin."

I asked, "Mind poling us toward the schooling bait while I ready the cast net?"

I descended from the poling platform and switched on the baitwell pump first, initiating the fill. Then I stepped onto the bow. Klinger took the pole and climbed the platform. I gripped the cast net's horn and doubled the slack over in my right hand. To untangle the quarter-ounce weights, I spread them across my left knee.

Off the bar, Klinger pointed to a healthy school no more than fifteen feet off the port side, in four feet of water. "Whole bunch, man … righ'over 'air."

"Just a little closer," I said. "I need another five-foot. They're just out of casting range."

"Want me toss one?" Klinger asked.

"Can handle it. Not my first time." Having tossed a cast for well over twenty years, a wise man would suggest a skill that I'd mastered, but not me.

Greenbacks, in the thousands, flipped and sent delicate vibrations throughout the water, drowning out all the other ambient sounds of nature.

Klinger pointed downward, feet from the bow. "Righ'ere. Toss it, Shamus!"

I cocked back and threw the net as though tossing a large mesh Frisbee. The cast net seemed to float in mid-air as Klinger used the push pole and pinned the boat, preventing a devastating drift over. Shaped like a banana, the net splashed into the water. Not my best cast. I pulled the leash, and Klinger poled the skiff back to assist in its closing.

"You got 'em," he said, descending from the poling platform.

I hauled the net closer and surprisingly, when I pulled the leash, it became clear that I'd trapped hundreds of twinkling baits. Using little effort, I stepped off the front portside deck.

Klinger said, "Look 'bout a hun'red piece."

I grabbed the cast net's horn, lifted, and guided the net alongside the gunwale. I heaved it into the boat atop the baitwell and released the frantic greenbacks. A lucky few immediately jumped to their freedom. I laid the net on the deck and reached for the dip net.

Klinger began clearing out the muck, as first mates do. After the water had cleared, we realized we'd caught some respectable bait indeed—perfect for the bull reds we were after.

"Try not to touch them," I said automatically to Klinger as he reached into the pile of bait.

"Who you tellin', son?"

"Sorry, charter guide habit."

Upon contact with the human fingertip, scale removal was evident, and why I preferred a no-touch process. Soon as the bait gets touched and scales slip free (not quite as bad as the threadfin), there were two ways it ends for the sardine: in the mouth of a carnivorous

Charlotte Harbor predator or inside a scale-filled, choke-friendly baitwell.

Klinger scooped up a large netload. "These're real nice. Real nice, Shamus."

"I'd say some of the nicest we've caught in a long time."

"Heck yeah. We should tear'id up, son!"

"I hope so. I know a few spots that have produced well as of late."

Klinger grinned. "Bet 'at Tur'le Bay fish shack is loaded up."

Five minutes later, hundreds of hardy greenbacks swam peacefully in the baitwell. I started the engine, and we idled off.

3

In the wheelhouse, aboard a twenty-four-foot Stamas named the *Itinerant*, stood a short, pudgy man who resembled a pear with two feet. His name was Lester, and his jowls hung low, drooping like the saddlebags on a horse. He wore stained, white overalls, a blue-striped shirt, and a green faded bucket-style fishing hat covering tin-colored hair.

A much taller man stood behind him with bulging, black, dove-like eyes, no hair, and he wore a black shirt that covered a barrel chest, and his camouflage pants had puffy cargo pockets.

Lester peered at a skiff through a pair of binoculars. "Those two look like they're headed in our direction … about five hundred yards out—two aboard, both male. The driver's hair is black, long, like a mop, and he's wearing a white visor, a white fishing shirt, and black shorts. There's a smaller man sitting ahead, wearing a red visor. His hair is a bit shorter, maybe blond. He's grown a goatee and mustache; sky-blue tank top, and he's wearing khaki shorts. Both wearing sandals... Are you getting all this?"

"Yup, yes, I am."

"Good, Eliot," Lester said. "That's good."

"Think they're headed our way?" Eliot asked.

"Could be. They're headin' in the direction of the Turtle Bay."

"They could be goin' anywhere," Eliot said. "There's a lot of water out here, plenty of spots to go. I know this harbor well. It's my home. Plus, they're fishermen anyways. See them rods?"

Lester lowered the binoculars that now hung below a doughy neck. "Yes, I see them."

"What time they droppin'?" Eliot asked.

"Should be in a few hours. They'll call when they're thirty minutes out."

"Are you sure this is legit?" Eliot asked. "Maybe we should cancel, get back to the dock, forget this ever happened."

"We can't, you fool—" Lester caught himself, continued, "Besides, don't you want the money? It's a fifty-fifty split. Five thousand apiece. All we do is scoop the delivery when it's flung out the plane and bring it ashore, then drop it off. Easy peasy. No big deal."

Eliot's voice cracked: "What if someone else get awn to it first?"

"*No one* will get to it first. That's why we're sitting here waiting for it. Why do you think they chose a Tuesday? Not as busy." He tapped a finger to his temple. "Think about it. Soon as we get the call, we move in."

"What's about those two in the skiff?"

"Didn't you just say that they're fishermen? The poles, remember?"

"Sure did, yes."

Lester held a cigarette between his yellow-stained fingers, taking a meaningful breath. "If anyone gets in our way, I'll take care of them, don't you worry about that." He shifted his arm, showed a shiny .38 tucked into his side pocket.

Eliot shook his head. "Whoa … whoa … whoa. You said no one was gettin' hurt!"

"If things go as planned, then no one *will* get hurt. Don't you want the money?"

"Yeah, I want it. I just don't want anyone gettin' hurt is all."

"You want to catch mullet the rest of your life? Or do you want to make some real cash, tax-free? I need to know you're in one hundred percent. If not, then you're a liability. If you want out, just say the word, and I'll keep the whole ten thousand, you can swim back to land." He pointed at the east wall, where it was more land accessible. "How'd you like that?"

"Okay, okay. I'm in."

Lester kept a hard stare into Eliot's eyes. "I want a guarantee. One hundred percent, no matter what?"

Eliot nodded. "I'm in."

"Good."

Eliot's nervousness caused him to rant. "I need the cash. You see, last week, over a few beers, a good bud Flip Peas and me was talking about mullet prices, and how they plummetin' and whatnot, and how fierce the competition is gettin', especially from these out-of-town fishermen. The net ban hurt our livelihoods. He mentioned on all the unfamiliar faces now sellin' mullet to our regular buyers … at a lower price, too. Local guys who'd been friends since childhood are now competitors, pitted against one another in the worst kinda ways … everyone's strainin' to make ends meet. Flip sounded right serious when tellin' me he might call it quits if the competition stays like it is. Friends of ours are already changin' fields, but for those of us who only know the water, our options are scarcer than a four-year-old scallop."

"Keep those thoughts to yourself, you hear?" Lester spun, pressed the binoculars back to his eyes and resumed watch; first the sky, then to the skiff at the two men aboard. He whispered, "Don't even think about getting in the way. Stay away, boys. Stay away."

4

After catching bait, I pointed the skiff toward Turtle Bay. The pelicans resumed feeding.

On portside, a sandbar, wherein the grass, a blue heron stalked tiny prey while the shadows of overhead gulls swept across the bow. Off starboard, mangrove shrubs, shallow beaches, long-dead mangrove trunks, and tiny no-see-ums lined the shore.

Turtle Bay's entrance was straight ahead—but first, the law required us to maintain a short distance of idle speed before entering, so I brought the skiff off plane.

I thought back to Klinger's rough appearance this morning. "Long night?"

"Ya'know it, man."

"What did you do?"

"W'ale … we started drinkin' at the house 'round four thir'y in the af'ernoon. Then 'round seven we headed awn up to Poons—me and Mandy. 'Course it was packed. They 'ad some cover band playin'. Could barely walk 'round wit' out bumpin' into someone. We drunk 'bout five drink 'piece … then 'round midnight Mandy start gettin' loud because someone spill'a drink on her, an' ya'know how 'at goes. So I figure it was time to get awn home. Got back to the house 'round midnight and passed out ..." He gripped his short chin hair. "...'bout two-thirty."

Klinger finished the bottled water, reached inside a pocket, and slung out a can of Copenhagen. "We seen 'at one girl yah jus' hired. You know ... for scrapin' boats." He added tobacco in a healthy pinch to his lower lip and his tongue packed it tight. "Wha's 'er name? Jenny?" He proceeded to spit out loose tobacco strands.

"Sara," I answered.

Sara Albright was the woman I had hired in recent times to help part-time with my dwindling bottom cleaning business.

"Yup, she was up 'air."

I shifted in the seat. "With who?"

"Looked like just some ol' friends to me. Hey, how'd yah find her anyways? She's real fine ... blonde hair, blue eye ... looks goo-ood."

"She's Jim's daughter, the guy I bought the truck from."

"Right, right. Good deal awn 'er?"

"I assume you mean the truck?"

"'Course, man."

"He wanted thirty-five hundred cash. I offered to trade my trailer, and he accepted. When I brought the trailer to his place a few days later, she was there. She mentioned that she just got back from college in Gainesville and looking for part-time work. I figured I could use a hand with the scraping business, so I mentioned it."

Klinger tightened the lipped chaw wad, tongue-compressed it. "I bet yooou did…" He spat and smiled.

"Funny."

"Ya'might want get with 'at, man."

"She's a nice girl."

"What's she, 'bout twenty-four, twenty-five-year-old?"

"Twenty-six."

"Okay—nice."

I eased with, "You *are* aware that she is an employee?"

"Yeah … I'm jus' sayin'…"

"Trust me, if something happens between Sara and me, you'll be the first to know."

Klinger pointed to the far-off stilted fish shack planted mid-way along the Turtle Bay shoreline. "We gonna hit 'at fish shack, right?"

I liked Klinger's enthusiasm, but the truth was, the spot was dead—over-fished.

"I fished it last time and didn't catch a thing. But we'll see…"

We both admired the water and approached the end of the NO WAKE
ZONE.

Klinger needed a spitter for his dip and thought an empty water bottle would work best.

"Do me a favor?" I asked. "Grab me some seeds from the cooler?"

Klinger's spirit remained high. "Here yah'r," he said.

I shoved in a handful, storing them in my cheek like a baseball player stores chaw.

We passed the NO WAKE marker, and back on plane, we disappeared into the backcountry. Entering a mangrove forest, we went on the notion of great expectations, more so after having filled our baitwell chock full of glossy, advantageous greenbacks.

My skiff was not super-fast like some of those rooster-tail shredding flats boats, equipping two hundred and fifty horsepower. I'm talking those gas-guzzling outboards—the ones skipping across the harbor shooting a twenty-foot-tall rooster tail as they speed upward of seventy miles per hour. No, no, my skiff was lightweight and designed to get back into the shallowest, sketchiest, nameless areas of Charlotte Harbor, ones that see very little action.

The air had a hazy morning lightness and breathed in with ease. The sun rose in elegance, peeking above the mangrove horizon, providing sufficient visibility both in and out of the water.

The old Turtle Bay fish shack stood pictorial a few hundred yards ahead. A simple box-shaped structure, it blended into the surrounding water, and the green bush beyond.

I adjusted the trim tabs, and the bow began to porpoise. The tide was insistent on returning, and mangroves bordering Turtle Bay disclosed gray, marl-covered oysters latched to roots of the green hedge.

I zoned out, envisioning an antiquated fish camp, maybe Calusa, maybe Clover, and in the center ... a campfire used for drying game skins overhung on a mangrove tree limb. Why not hunters floating nearby in subsistence-minded dugout canoes? I zoned back in.

The weather, although forecasted to become muggy, lingered in our favor for the time being, but the ever-present threat of afternoon thunderstorms remained my top concern.

As we coated, mangrove islands, one after the other, emerged after each corner. Ahead, plump odd-eyed mullet breached, shooting through the air, two, three times in a row—a brilliant morning.

Soon after, a startled cormorant dove violently from a branch into the limpid seawater. Klinger pointed to its arrow-shaped head, sporting a curved beak tip. It popped up and glanced back while it swam away in utter annoyance.

We continued to skim the backcountry's grass flats, passing over sand hole after sand hole, scattering numerous species of fish. Ahead, the tip of a mangrove overhang housed a school of fish loafing inches under the water's surface, just shy of the fish shack. I throttled back, and the skiff slowed to idle.

I pointed toward it. "See that school over there?"

Klinger snatched his fishing rod and said, "Dem look like reds."

I leaned the push pole against the rod holder attached to the platform and climbed it. "Get ready. I'm going to get us a bit closer. Don't cast right on them. Wait till I say, okay?" My guide habits unconsciously carried over to personal trips.

Klinger released the hook from the eyelet saver on his 7'6" medium-heavy rod above the corked grip. He opened the baitwell, reaching for a greenback, and went to hook it through the nose.

"Wait," I said. "Try tail hooking it."

"You an 'at dang tail hookin'…"

"Yes, trust me. It will go at least twenty foot further." I spat an empty sunflower shell into the water, then tightened and swallowed the juice.

The school of fish was indeed redfish—big ones. Under the tree, they loafed then fed, loafed then fed, nose down, tail up, exposing a prehistoric eye. Klinger and I were now within casting range. I dug the pole deep and tied it off, preventing any unwanted drift.

Klinger dipped the baitfish in the water. "Now?" he asked.

"Hang on," I whispered. "Okay, see if you can get to the right of them, away from the mangroves."

A quick whip of the rod and the greenback slung through the air like a missile on its way to an intended target. It landed fifteen feet outside the school—a perfect cast.

"Nice!" I said.

A new arrival was sensed. A weighty predatory specimen shot out from the school, pushing its own wake. The hungry redfish darted toward the bait like a killer whale attacking seals on a beach. The baitfish sensed trouble, *big trouble*, and with a last-ditch attempt, flipped its whole body from the water over and over, trying to gain an advantage, but it was too late—it was just too late.

"He's on it!" I shouted.

The redfish gulped the bait down and darted back to the transitory school. The line sliced the water like a wire through wet clay—effervescent tendrils trailed behind.

Klinger set the hook—a fearless jerk, and the drag on his 4000 series Shimano Spheros screamed to life. In short pulses, the fish stripped off many yards of good line. The fleeting school broke apart—huge fish scattered all around us.

A heron flew away, squawking from a nearby branch, launching a warning that an intruder was close.

Klinger's rod flexed back near the breaking point. He stood—sea legs now unaffected by an assumed hangover, his voice soaring to a high-pitched, enthusiastic croak. "There she is, son!"

I descended from the poling platform. "Tighten your drag!"

"I'm tryin', man."

Smooth clicks indicated Klinger tightening the drag.

I cracked a wise ass smile. "We might have to chase if you can't stop him."

The fish shot toward the mangroves, then toward the fish shack hulking on starboard. Klinger continued cranking and pulling up. The fish surfaced, a momentary donation of its size—a nice bull red.

"I'd say he's over slot," I said.

"Yeah, buddy!"

I readied the landing net. "What do you think, oversized?"

Klinger breathed heavy. "Su-ure feel like it."

I figured it was a good time for a joke. "You're not tired, are you?"

He cranked on the reel, lips tight. "Not'a damn chance, this one's mine!"

While he ratcheted in the redfish, it became clear this monster would measure well over the twenty-seven-inch legal limit.

I told him, "Swing it over here, head-first. I'll use the net and scoop."

The fish flipped its tail, ripping more line from the reel.

"Not sure she done yet!" Klinger bowed the rod to the fish. "Easy now, big fella."

"How's the lead?" I lowered the net into the water. "Good shape?"

"She bar'ly hangin' awn."

I was proud of my friend. Hard not to get enthused when fishing alongside Klinger.

"Nice fish!" I said.

"Look 'bout thirty-plus inch." Klinger eased the redfish to the surface, where the tight line made a sound similar to a guitar's high E.

"There she is," he said. "She a monster, Shamus."

I noticed that the hook held the fish by only a delicate portion of thin, white lip, so I rushed in, scooped up the fish, and lowered it atop the deck. "That's a beautiful looking fish. Nice catch."

Klinger marveled at the enormous thing, as did I.

After a few deep breaths, he said, "Whoa, 'ats the biggest red I ever caught. How big yah think she is?"

"At least thirty-four inches, maybe thirty-five. Untangle it from the net and we'll see."

Using focus, and a wettened hand, Klinger removed the fish from the net and detached the hook. "Look'at that?" he said, noticing how close he came to losing the redfish. "She barely hangin'awn."

I laid the thirty-six-inch measuring stick onto the deck. "Lay it down here."

Klinger laid the redfish overtop the stick and blinked. "She's thirty-five inch!"

"Wow, that's a great fish," I said, hinting jealousy. "Hold it up. I'll take a picture for you."

I took his phone out and opened the camera.

"Good thinkin', Shamus."

Klinger used magical powers and settled the pretty fish enough to secure it and pose for a picture.

I said, "Say…low seas and fair weather."

Klinger held the redfish, stretching his smile. He nearly lost grip, but was able to ask, "Get'er?"

"Yup, sure did. Better lower it back in the water and revive it."

Klinger lowered the fish into the water like laying a sleeping baby into its crib. The tail of the redfish began swaying back and forth, gaining strength—its black prehistoric tail eye blinking back at us, scales glinting red in the morning light. After the fight, it surprised me that the fish had any strength left at all.

Klinger swayed the redfish back and forward, streaming oxygen-rich water through its throbbing red gills. It gained purpose and willpower in a matter of seconds and its head shook, telling Klinger it was ready to leave the two of us behind. The fish swam off without a second look. Like a memory, it disappeared into the thick, tangled seagrass.

Klinger checked his reel for burn marks.

I said, "Great fight, really."

Klinger stood tall on the bow, full of accomplishment. "Thank yah, man. 'At was insane! T'bad she over slot."

His redfish was too large to keep, passing the twenty-seven-inch max, and so we had no choice but to release it. I encouraged the clients I chartered to also release their catch, even if it met the legal requirements.

Klinger said, "I'm sendin'is pic to Mandy righ'now. Make sure she knows who catch the *fish* in this fam'ly. Ya'got m'phone?"

"Yeah, it's right here." I opened the phone and pretended to check the photos. "Oh no! I think I deleted the picture by accident, sorry."

Klinger cried out in panic. "Shamus … no! You serious?"

I could not resist a quick jab. "No, I got it right here." I had to hold back, not to burst into laughter.

"C'mon, man … 'at ain't cool." He swiped the phone from my hand. "Mandy'll be so proud of me. Migh'even gi'me some buns." He shook his head as if he had just solved some sort of an enigma. After sending the picture, he stuffed the phone down his khaki's pocket.

"Buns?" I asked. "How many kids do you have now?"

He recollected—then grinned. "Five … five kids."

"Nice."

Klinger skipped off the deck and snatched open the cooler. "Yah know wha' time it is?"

I knew.

"Beer thirty!" He popped open a can of beer. "Yah want one?"

"I'm not dead, am I?"

Klinger spun the can to the proper spot, and his annunciation was on point. "Cheers to you, man."

I held out the can. "Cheers."

The ice-cold beer went down by the gulp. I sat back, gazed ahead at the heat waves glimmering off the distant stagnant water. The first drop of sweat left my forehead, making way to my temple. A sweltering day was imminent. While we finished our rewards, I wanly lifted out of the chair and climbed atop the poling platform to scope for the school. It was nowhere in sight.

"They're long gone now," I said.

Klinger leaped onto the bow, arms spread wide, extended backward, and let out an impressive belch. "Sure look like it." He couldn't hold back the urge and unzipped his shorts, pressed the can to his lips, bent back, gulped beer, and began pissing off the boat. "Yes, sir."

5

After a brief intermission, I pressed down on the push pole, propelling us toward the Turtle Bay fish shack.

Schooled together on the surface, a hundred mullet exposed thin dorsal fins like miniature sailboats. Still, even with our presence, they vaulted through the air, slap-landing on their sides. If I were given a dollar every time a charter client had asked me why mullet did these strange aerobatic maneuvers, I'd be a rich man. It's said mullet breach the water to break apart egg sacks in their belly. I'd also heard they do it to rid their skin of parasites.

Klinger now inspected his monofilament leader line.

I soaked in the beauty and enjoyed the moment.

Klinger finished his leader-line scrutiny and shot a cast toward a bushel of red mangrove roots.

The waxed line shot off the reel—*fsssssss*. Then the soft click of the closing bail echoed across the water.

Jigging the bait, he asked, "So why'd yah decide to sell 'at ol' trailer?"

"It was getting little use," I said. "Just sitting there on the side of the garage, rotting away next to the

Wrangler. And frankly, I didn't have near that kind of cash. I got lucky Mr. Albright decided to make the trade."

"I hear it. If I had known ya'was sellin' her, I woulda taken it off yah hands."

"For two grand?"

"Shamus, we could'a came up wid'a fair enough price."

"I think two grand is a fair price. I paid five grand for it ten years ago."

He made another cast. "Might 'ave overpaid, bud."

I gripped the push pole and then jolted the skiff, breaking Klinger's balance on the bow, an attempt to dunk him into the water.

"Nice try!" He smiled, stepped back, and then mocked a cast as if tempting me to do it again.

I continued poling us through the grass flats and over numerous sand holes in pursuit of predatorial fish in hopes we'd spot a few extra fish before lunch.

Klinger completed cast after cast toward the fringes of single grass clumps, coming up empty. We approached the fish shack. A small mangrove forked skyward, reaching for the sun at the base of a structural piling. Just before that, a dead mangrove log jutted out, extending weathered branches upward as long, black, witch-like fingers.

I nodded toward the long-dead log. "Give that a shot."

Klinger made a whopping cast, a tremendous attempt, overshooting the log and hitting the pilling, then into the forked sprout of new mangroves.

"Boy, did 'at one get 'way from me. Mus' be 'at tail hookin'. He cracked a grin and scratched his blond head.

I smiled and push poled us toward the shrubbery. Klinger jerked the rod, shaking the mangrove branch.

"You see it?" I asked.

"Over'air." He whipped the rod, sending handfuls of yellow, sacrificial leaves to float atop the water in bliss.

I noticed a taut line. "Can you reach it?"

Klinger knelt on the bow like a hunting dog, tugging the line. "Sure, jus' get'er awn in a bit closer."

"There's a bunch of stumps in the way."

"C'mon, man. Lil' farther."

I bumped the boat a tick forward. "You good? Need a hand?"

"'Air she is," he said.

"You got it?"

"Nah, she pretty far back."

He kept reaching in, bending back mangrove branches. I pushed him up under the fish shack. Using pliers, he extracted the hook from the red-skinned mangrove root as though it were a tooth.

"Got it!" He presented the hook like a trophy. "'At hook was buried way deep." His attention went to underneath the shack's floorboards.

"What are you looking at?" I asked.

"Hatch."

"What hatch?"

Klinger had his neck twisted up, as though looking up a chimney fluke. "All 'ese shacks have 'em."

The fish shack had once served primarily as an icehouse, storing tons of ice to chill the plentiful catches brought in by fishermen of days long past. It still stood solid along the western bank of Turtle Bay, a sizable structure of roughly five hundred square feet. A tin roof sheltered it, while light filtered through wooden awning-style windows. The exterior finish was a spotty-at-best stucco job, and small pecker holes scattered throughout the haphazardly spread mud. Attached without the use of a ledger board and held up by frail brittle two-by-fours, and angling outward, a half-rotted narrow deck wrapped its entire perimeter.

I reversed us.

Satisfied, Klinger reached into his khaki pocket and out came a crumpled spliff.

"Breakfast?" I asked.

Klinger lit the spliff and pulled long and strong. He held the smoke in, replied, "Yeah buddy," and exhaled.

"Grab me a water?"

The spliff slipped to the corner of his mouth, and he removed a dripping wet water bottle from the cooler.

I took it. "Ahh," I said, with the refreshing cold grip of chilled water.

Klinger handed the spliff my way, raising a brow, and a smile. "Still cuttin' back?"

Any special occasion, like Klinger's morning over-slot redfish, required some sort of celebration, and when Klinger offered, I accepted. I received the spliff in happiness, took a pull, and returned it. I drank another slug of beer, sat in the captain's chair, leaned back, and enjoyed the sun.

"Let's try this cut up 'air … star'berd, using some live ones." Klinger took another hit, added, "Look deep enough ta'old *some* fish."

I noticed my friend's interesting cut, and since it required no effort on my part, I stretched my hands behind my head, interlocked my fingers, flung my feet up onto the console, I said, "Good observation. Pole us over."

"Thir'y minute, man. 'At's the rule."

"Thirty minutes? What rule?"

He breathed out smoke. "They'll bite again after thir'y minute."

"Where? Here?"

"Ye-up."

Under the brim of his visor, Klinger ashed-out the spliff and eased it down his pocket. If I knew my friend, at some point, that spliff would make another appearance. He snagged the push pole and coasted us forward.

We were twenty yards north of the fish shack when Klinger set the push pole deep in the sand, lowered his voice to a whisper, and locked his attention on the future fishing hole. "We'll shoot back to 'at shack in a sec. But for now, I bet'er some *nice* ones in this cut." He hopped down from the poling platform.

I leaned back, and things happened.

He opened the baitwell and tried to scoop bait.

I began getting pumped. "Chum up a bit," I suggested. "Just the little guys. Save the big ones for later." More chartering logic.

Klinger swept the net deep into the well and removed it full of bait.

Rapid, hysterical, motor-like flapping told us that the bait was very desperate to flee.

Klinger proceeded to the bow, squeezing the loaded net, setting off a high-pitched squeak. During chartering, I liked to squeeze the bait lightly. It leads them to the surface, swimming circularly, and with luck, triggers fish in the vicinity to strike.

Klinger then asked, "Where 'at bait launcher?"

"In the front hatch, underneath your feet."

I'd manufactured a homemade bait slinger using an old plastic toy bat I'd found lying abandoned on the side of the road. I sliced a thirty-degree chunk off the top, giving the bait a nice lip to launch from.

He apprehended the bait and loaded the launcher— then cocked back and let it fly like he was back in little league. A dozen baits flew out, some hitting just the right angle, darting through the air. Others hit the mangroves, fell through bushes, pinged off roots, and dropped into the water. But most hit the surface, scattering like a handful of tossed rocks.

"Nice shot," I said, waiting, anticipating. The lucky little baits—or not so lucky—swam in circles, summoning each other, desperate to be pressed into a safe and secure pod.

My eyes lowered to a single, flickering bait, eagerly swimming back toward the boat, searching for shelter. It swam underneath and disappeared. A few, after the brunt of Klinger's squeeze, swam on their sides in tiny circles.

Part of me felt bad for them. Could I save them? They seemed to be doomed from the day they were hatched, which happened with most things, I suppose. A lucky few might end up finding fleeting refuge deep in the tangled grass, but ravenous fish would find them soon enough. I wondered if they had any other purpose on Earth than to feed other fish—or the occasional human? They swim in pods just waiting to get eaten, right? Schools of wolfing fish migrate with them, following the pods for miles, stalking on the fringes for a chance to dart in and feed. They were almost irresistible to gluttonous predatory fish like snook, redfish, and tarpon. Alive or cut to chunks, doesn't matter. Plunking a hardy greenback ahead of any one of those fish will initiate a strike. They can't resist it—they won't resist it. The baitfish fluttered on the surface, and I wondered what rested beneath the water of such a murky cut.

From a distance, I heard Klinger shouting, "Shamus … Shamus … *SHAMUS!*"

I snapped from a daze. "Yeah … what's up?"

"Are yah okay?" he asked, smiling.

"You was zoned out, man."

"I sure was, and you ruined it. What's in this stuff? I don't remember spliffs being this strong. You smoke this stuff all day long?"

"Sure do, man … keeps t'Boogeyman away."

"I got to hand it to you." I again shook my head. "You might be the man. I knew you smoked all day, but this stuff? That's seriously potent. Back in the day, all we smoked was *regs*. Mexican fart dust, we called it." I shifted. "Not anywhere close to this stuff."

"Not sure wha'ta tell yah, Shamus. You a lightweight. It's a toler'ance thing. Gotta build yours back up, man. Me and Mandy smoke this daily. Have been f'years."

"I'm not sure what to tell me either," I said, but pointed my face to the underwater movement triggered by our chummed greenbacks.

As the helpless creatures swam on, I focused on the clouds—saw one in the shape of a man's face, wearing a handlebar mustache, and another, a space shuttle.

High above, an eagle soaring through the clouds buzzed like a mechanical bird. How could an eagle make a sound like that? I recognized that sound. That wasn't the eagle at all. It was a plane's propeller slicing through the air, and it was low—and close.

6

I n the sky, a single-engine plane flying nearly at water level, skimmed the tallest mangrove branches, then began to circle.

"You see that, Klinger?"

"Hell yeah, man. I's an air-o-plane."

I nodded.

"Thing low, huh?"

"Yes, way too low." I stood and headed to the bow, still a bit stoned.

Klinger stared up, blocking the sun with his hand. "Why yah think it's flyin' so dang low for?"

"Not sure," I said, speaking in a sober tone, or so I thought. "Its elevation seems too low for this area, and aviation rules in general. Charlotte County Airport is ten miles away. This isn't good. He might be experiencing mechanical problems and going down." I checked the front hatch for a medical kit.

"I don't see no smoke," Klinger said. "Engine's runnin'. I'can hear it. Sounds normal t'me, I guess."

Klinger was right. The plane sounded normal, strong engine, no sputter, no signs of a stall. After coming up empty with the medical kit, another unlicensed misstep, I picked out a twelve-gauge flare gun, just in case. After reading the package, the flare read past the safe, useable date, but I loaded one anyway and tucked it down my waist. Being an unlicensed captain required no bothersome Coastie inspections, but I now ran the risk of firing a dud.

Klinger asked, "Yah shootin' a flare at it, man?"

"Of course not. I'm keeping it right next to me, just in case."

"Oh…"

"It sounds like it's coming back, and they may need help, so be ready."

Klinger's calm demeanor seemed abnormal for the situation. Maybe it was the spliff, maybe it was me who started to overreact.

Klinger head swiveled toward the clouds. "I's gone, Shamus … don't 'ear it no more."

My head angled up and down. "I still hear it."

In the short distance, this time, the plane flew even lower, a direct flight above the boat, approaching us at full speed.

I ducked. "Here it comes!"

A violent gust from the propeller blew the visor off my head and into the water.

"Holy damn!" I yelled.

"My God, man!"

Just as fast as the plane flew beyond us, it disappeared behind the mangroves, spreading them apart like a mini-tornado—twisting and turning, separating the branches.

Klinger's chest was pulsating. "Jesus, man. You see 'at? It look like an old beat up plane t'me … see 'at rust on the underside? Them doors were open, too … or did it even 'ave doors?"

"Not exactly sure. The fuselage did have rust on it, huh?" I reached into the water to retrieve my visor. "Are you sure the doors were open?"

"Heck yeah, man. It *definitely* had'er doors open."

"Did you see anyone inside—any movement?"

Klinger's thin voice created the vibe. "Think I seen the pilot … before it dis'peared behind 'em mangroves." He pointed north.

"Maybe someone's test flying an old beater plane out of Charlotte County Airport?"

"I sure don't know, man. Somethin' veeeery strange 'bout this."

"What's strange about an aircraft in distress?" I said, gazing out toward the direction of the plane. "Happens all the time..."

When I shook my visor, the water spun from it like drops slinging off a wet dog. I put it back on, tasting the salt-filled water as it dripped off the bill, down my nose, and into my mouth.

Klinger pointed northeast toward the mouth of Turtle Bay. "Maybe we should move awn over 'at open area, over 'air. Get us a better look."

The more I thought about it, the more it made sense that the plane might need our help.

"They could be signaling us for some reason. Check your cell signal for me, would you?"

Klinger jammed a hand inside his pocket and slung out a cell phone, and then held it high to the sky. "Nope, big ol' nothin'…"

"No signal?"

"Zero, man … nada."

I checked my phone. "Mine neither." A boatload of urgency approached. I caved. "Okay, let's go. Reel your line up, and let's head over—see if we can at least get a better view."

Before I could utter another word, Klinger, already ahead of me, began to speed-reel his line tight. "Sound good, man." He set the rod in the rod holder on the side console. "Is excitin', man! Wha' if 'at plane crashes and we gotta kick it into rescue mode?"

I jerked the push pole from the muck and locked it into the gunwale hooks. "Let's hope we don't have to kick *it* into *any* mode." I started the engine and set it to idle. The mystery factor was building. Adrenalin began oozing into my bloodstream.

Klinger paid close attention and positioned himself on the bow, on all fours—a ready-for-takeoff position. "It look deep 'nough, I'll say."

"We'll see," I said, to keep Klinger on his toes. "Be ready."

"Always."

Before leaving, the sky caught my attention. "Clouds are building—rain's in our future."

"Florida, man. It's life…"

I adjusted the jack plate at four inches and set my trim tabs to the downward position—we were ready.

The skiff lifted off when I hammered the throttle, using its semi-vee hull to split the water with surprising ease. The trim tabs needed a readjustment, which lifted the bow. Suddenly, the engine's foot began digging along bottom, so I used the jack plate to lift it, clearing the friction from the skeg. Free from drag, I trimmed the engine to the cruise position, decreasing cavitation, thus, sending the boat on a smooth, engine-efficient plane, aiming us toward Turtle Bay, and after the aircraft.

<u>7</u>

Aboard the *Itinerant*, the shorter of the two men, Lester Smith, gaped to the sky, waiting for a sign.

The delivery was scheduled for ten o'clock a.m. or thereabouts—night was not an option. The plane flew blind, no navigational equipment, no radar—no nothing. Straight from Mariel Harbor, Cuba, all the way to Florida.

Lester tilted his head, admiring the darkening clouds. "They should be here any second now."

The hulking Eliot sat in a plastic lawn chair and was rocking on the mound of his big toe. "I've a bad feelin' about this. Somethin' don't feel right."

Lester snapped, "Feel right? Something don't *feel* right? Don't tell me you're losing your spine? You said you are in one hundred percent. No backing out now."

"Nope, I'm not backin' out. I'm just sayin' that somethin' don't feel right."

"When we're done with this job, you tell me how five thousand dollars feels, okay?" Lester slid off the hat and wiped the sweat from a fissured forehead. "You better not clam up on me…"

"I'm not one to clam up. I need that money very much. I got bills to pay too, yah know? I got kids wantin' to go to college. I really ought to replace my old net, the one I lost on an oyster bed last week—it's my main one, and I use it often. That's 'bout two hundred and fifty dollars right there. The bank's about to levy my account and damn-near to foreclosin' on my house unless I get current with the mortgage. I need this money. I got no other options."

Lester said, "Thoughts to yourself, remember? Do what I say, when I say it, and we'll be outta here just after dark."

Eliot was surprised. "After dark?"

"Yes, after dark. That's when we high-tail it back to the dock. The plan is to wait for the drop, retrieve the package, lay low back in … um … what's the name again? Turtle Bay, that's it. We lay low for a few hours until the second call comes in that the pick-up guy has arrived, which shouldn't be long after dark. They don't want to move during the day. Ponce de Leon Park closes at dusk, remember? The city will lock the park up real tight. That's where we're to bring the package. There'll be a car waiting to take what we bring back, see? Should be all but deserted at that time, less chance of getting seen. We take our cash and split, got it?"

"Yeah, I got it," Eliot said.

Lester's tone softened, satisfying, as if winning an argument. "Gooood."

Eliot breathed in deep, turning back toward the harbor; he scanned across the water's unctuous surface, toward Turtle Bay using the binoculars. His phone rang. The piano intro to the song *Your Love Broke Through*, by Keith Green, split the silence.

Lester rolled his eyes when he recognized the song. "Here we go..."

Eliot blinked at him, pulled the phone from his pocket, flipped it open, and read the caller ID.

"Well?" Lester had little serenity. "Are you answering it?"

Eliot's trembling hand transferred the phone over. "You answer it," he said.

Lester brought it to his ear and raised his chin, summoning what little courage he had. "Hello? … uh-huh … right … okay. We're in place … uh-huh. Cape Haze Point, yes … can't miss us." He snapped the phone closed. "It's on its way."

Eliot swallowed hard, thumping to the bow to check the anchor, signaled an all-tight thumbs-up to the wheelhouse when he finished securing it, but whispered to himself, "Oh Lord Jesus, what have I got myself into? Partnerin' up with this guy, what was I thinkin'? Just stick to the plan and things will go smooth as a dolphin's back." Eliot climbed to the wheelhouse. "Towing that Whaler'll on the way back'll sure slow us down a bit."

"You don't worry about that," Lester said. "The Whaler is brand new. It will be just fine. Plus, how do you propose we travel back in those shallows? This ol' broad drafts two feet. The little boat's good for the skinny waters and back again."

Eliot resisted at first, then nodded. "Understood, yup."

Lester handed the binoculars to Eliot. "Make yourself useful and take these binoculars and look out for the plane, okay?"

Eliot brought them to his eyes and peered through to the sky. "Nothing."

"You probably won't see anything for a little while now." Lester shook his head derisively. "We only have about four miles of visibility but keep an eye out, just in case. You want to look toward the southwest, that's where they're coming from."

"Okay. Storm's a buildin'."

Lester reached inside his breast pocket, pulled out a pack of Menthol 305s, shook one out, and set it between his teeth. His chapped lips pressed on to it, then he lowered the pack, releasing the cigarette. He lit it using a Zippo. "If this goes well there could be more of these opportunities to come, if you're interested..." The smoke blew out, cyclonic as it was forced between chapped lips.

Eliot pressed the binoculars to his eyes. His chest filled with a sigh while searching for the two fishermen toward Turtle Bay. "I think this might be it for me. I don't need to be caught up in all this illegal business. I just want to make a quick dollar and catch up with bills is all—then I'm out."

"Out?" Lester was doubtful.

"Yeah, out," Eliot repeated. "This here is a one-time event for me, I think."

"Who said anything about illegal?" An extensive pull off his cigarette was necessary while he stared into Eliot's eyes. "You're just thinking about it too much. You gotta relax a little. This job is no big deal. Plus, it pays well for just one day's work, right?"

Eliot eyed the pocket-stuffed gun in the pair-shaped man's suspenders. "Yeah, it might pay well ... we'll see, I suppose." He then thought, *I should have never agreed to this job. Once we make the drop, I want nothin' to do with this guy. At least I've got my lord and savior, Jesus Christ on my side. Damn Flip for linking me to this man. I had no idea this was the side job. I figured it was somethin' legal, like movin' boats or scrapin' bottoms. Not this ... I didn't sign up for this.*

Eliot tried to siphon more information, so he turned toward Lester. *Please Jesus, I find strength in you.* "Where's this plane comin' from anyhow?"

"From Cuba. I told you never mind that ... the less you know, the better. I'll worry about the details, okay?" Lester nodded toward the stern. "You want to check those Whaler lines?"

Eliot left the wheelhouse and hurried down the three-rung ladder, to the stern of the boat. From where the Whaler had been tied, he moved toward the cleat and tugged at the tow lines using little effort. He contemplated boarding the Whaler, cutting the line, motoring back to the ramp, ditching the boat, and forgetting all about this, never to deal with Lester again. He mumbled, "I need the money. Jesus, if you can hear me, I could use a sign. Tell your father ol' Eliot is here and needs a hand." He paused, listened—but nothing, and continued in a soft whisper, "It's okay, I know you're a busy man." He finished with a thought: *Let's just see how it goes. One slight hint of danger and I'm gone.*

After inspecting the lines, he glanced at Lester, who was peering intently out of the *Itinerant's* broken cabin window.

Eliot observed the stained brown fiberglass deck. The cracks, filled in black grime, ran like spiderwebs along the greasy deck. Oxidation had begun on each piece of chrome-plated hinge, on every zinc plated screw. He muttered, "A little polish couldn't hurt." Underneath the plastic lawn chair he'd sat on earlier, a red tackle box caught his attention. He again checked Lester. Over to it, he knelt and expanded the top trays outward.

"Everything tight?" Lester called from the wheelhouse without taking his eyes off the harbor.

"Yeah—yeah, all tight." Eliot cleared his throat, froze, and didn't look up, but perceived a faded, "Good," from the wheelhouse.

He rummaged through the tackle box, discovered a knife; a rusted, red-handled, fish scale-encrusted bait knife. He pressed his eyes shut and opened a puffed camouflaged cargo pocket, charily slipping the knife inside. "Just in case."

8

We hit top speed in nearly the length of five boats, the engine revving hard but muffled beneath the cowling as I eased the throttle forward.

Klinger's arms flew up, and he shouted something toward the eastern wall of Cape Haze Point. "'Air it is!"

"You're way too excited for this," I said above the drone of engine.

"Yeah, buddy."

"You know it might be horrifying if the plane goes down and crashes, right? Are you ready if we need to kick it into rescue mode or potentially … recovery mode?"

"Ain't no thing, man." He centered his sight, found the plane in the sky, pointed, and blurted, "I see it!"

The plane flew low still, and without any comprehensible damage, it circled, lapping Cape Haze Point—a mangrove neck of land forty acres in total and lavishly filled in dense mangrove thickets, copious in swamp marl, and further back, a spread of salt marsh flats. One side sits Charlotte Harbor, and the other, Turtle Bay. We were a long five minutes out.

Ahead, the low-circling plane suddenly flushed twenty pelicans out from their sitting posts, an inconvenience to the birds, who flew off, far from the noisy plane.

Then an object fell from the aircraft. Something had broken off and began to plunge, to land deep, centered within the peninsula.

Klinger turned and shrieked ahead of the center console, "Did yah see 'at, Shamus? I think something jus' fell from 'at plane!"

I studied the plane. If it descended or began nosediving in a fiery smoking hell, our plans would change. Maybe it would at least signal MAYDAY—but nothing.

I put the throttle to neutral, and the skiff collapsed off plane, plowing to a stop. "You see that?" I said with a hint of sketch. "Did something seriously just fall out of it?"

Klinger whispered, "Dude, I think someone jus' got thrown outta 'at plane and into t'funk … in 'ose mangrove thickets." He pointed.

"Are you *sure* it was a person?" I asked. "It could've been a piece of the plane, a door, something..."

"Don't know, man."

"Can you be *sure*?"

Klinger's eyes widened. "Had'a parachute though."

"What?"

"Yup, didn't look 'ike it did much help, though. Har'ly even opened."

"I doubt it was a person then..."

Klinger remained skeptical. "Ehh—don't know, man."

"Did you see a head?"

"Um … not too sure on 'at one neither."

I needed more. Even though I'd seen it, I wasn't comprehending. "What did you see, Klinger?"

He couldn't contain his angst. "I saw somethin' fall from 'at plane. I'm sure of it. May not 'ave been a body, but it was pretty big and had the same dang shape! Maybe wid'out the limbs, though—and the parachute."

As Klinger bit his nails, I fixated up at the plane. It no longer circled but set on a heading locked toward Boca Grande Pass.

We both sat still, and in our own way, processed what was happening.

As jacked up as Klinger acted, he had processed the info a lot quicker than me. He shot to his feet while we blasted over the flats of Turtle Bay sound. "Let's go check 'at thing out!"

I felt to pull back on my own interest, to even out Klinger's excitement, maybe to establish some sort of captain-like dominance, so I added a slight edge to the tone. "I'm not sure… That might have been meant for someone else, *not* us."

Klinger attention glued onto the plane. "I's leavin', look!"

I couldn't hide my inflating, audible interest, because deep within me, I wanted to see what had fallen. "Looks to be going somewhere…"

"Let's get awn over and check it out, man!" Klinger's mental amperage had reached maximum levels, and he couldn't be influenced otherwise. "Might be a big ol' pile of money or somepin, huh?"

I found the blip of the plane fading in the distance. "That's the last thing I hope it is. If it is money, we'd be in *deep* if we stole it, you dig?"

Klinger settled into the seat ahead of the center console, turned to me. "If it is money, hear me out. We take it, 'en bring it awn back for a big ree-ward. Yeah, 'at's what w'can do!"

"Bring it back?" I asked. "Where exactly do we bring it to?"

"I don't know—brin' to the cops?"

I tried, "Yeah, right. They'd ask all sorts of questions. Interview this, interview that. And Shamus Pickford is no rat—forget it."

"Man … I cou'd use a few ex'ra bucks…"

I shook off Klinger's nonsense at this point, geared the engine, and idled toward the peninsula's tip. Whatever it was, it had fallen a tick north of Cape Haze Point, centered on the deepest, muggiest, no-see-um-loaded, half-submerged area around.

Finally, I said, "If it's money, we leave it and get the hell out of there."

"Okay, okay. Here, let's a'least swing on over 'air and see if w'can even get to it, okay?"

I finally caved in trepidation. "Fine."

Numerous twisting creeks and cuts lined the inside wall of Turtle Bay, none of which, at the current tide, had any sort of usable depth. We continued a sketchy idle along to the region where the package had fallen to search for the easiest entry point.

Klinger pointed into the green bush. "Look 'ike she dropped 'round 'ere, man."

"Not sure we can make it back there from where we are now," I said. "We may have to go in farther. Nowhere to stand anywhere I see."

Klinger's focus remained steadfast on the mangroves. "Sure is, man. I seen big ol' wild salt hogs back in 'ese mangroves b'fore. They gotta walk on somepin…"

I still didn't share Klinger's excitement. "Salt hogs? Greaaat…" I mumbled.

Klinger reached inside a pocket, removed a can of Copenhagen. "No, really, man. Me and my ol' man fished back 'ere 'bout two year ago, and a big ol' three hun'red pounder came right out'n swam cross this last creek up here on the lef'." He paused for effect. "Saw it wit my own eyes."

My memory returned. "I believe you. I forgot they litter Cape Haze Peninsula, and I've heard from friends who say they've seen salt hogs out here." I thought briefly. "It was that Desoto guy who brought them damn things here. I'd hate to run across one, though." I took time to test my old friend. "What do you suggest … if we do come up on one of those things?"

"How I know?" Klinger replied sharply.

"I thought you knew all about those damn things?"

"I sure know how 'en *eat* 'em."

"Salt hogs?"

"Yea, but they don't taste as good … as 'em inland hogs."

I began to get hungry.

The chaw packed in his lower lip weighed it down, exposing a few bottom teeth. "There's nothin' to 'em, really. They *will* charge at yah, 'ats for sure."

Now I started rethinking the whole plan. "You're not making me feel comfortable with this. I don't want to surprise the hell out of a big lone male."

"You'be fine. Sure can smell 'em big ones when they get close, so…"

We idled parallel, two hundred feet off dense, humid mangroves when a distant thunderhead rumbled. I pulled my phone from the dry box and checked the weather. No signal.

The source of the thunder faced south—an impressive storm building in the distance near Pine Island Sound, stretching miles into the sky as though looking up a mountainside at snow-covered peaks.

Afternoon thunderstorms in South Florida were some of the fiercest in the country. To get tangled in one was the last thing I wanted. We needed to get in, verify no one needed help, and get out—quick. Part of me wanted to leave right then and return to fishing—say *screw* this, but the other half—the curious half—craved to check the thing out. And a potential pile of cash.

We continued idling along the mangroves until our arrival at the last starboard creek. It had been thirty minutes since we witnessed the drop.

Klinger perched on the bow. "Try 'is one, man."

I clenched the stainless-steering wheel. "Keep an eye out for oyster beds."

On the bow, Klinger stared downward, holding the blue bow rope. "All clear so far, man."

As we entered the creek, I mentally noted our exact path.

Klinger pressed the rope between his legs and cupped his hands to the sides of his sunglasses, to block the peripheral sunrays. "Keep 'er goin' straight, man— stay on this path. Look like w'got some shallow spots comin' up soon … on the lef'."

Exposed mounds of million-year-old sand littered Klinger's area of interest. Though not large enough to be anything serious, we continued navigating in caution. Over time, it became a chore to avoid the plumes of mud deposits and the abundant long-dead stumps.

A blue heron, spooked from a branch, squawked and took flight. The current tidal height tide still exposed plenty of red-barked mangrove roots, indicating the water would soon return. Some sun, semi-blocked by rain-soaked, compressing clouds, was there, high in the sky, continuing onward with its westward quest. Short gusts of wind veered around bends, sweeping ripples across the topmost layer of the sea.

Klinger and I had wound a quarter of a mile into a magnificent, sweet-smelling, mangrove fortress, green on all sides, and denser than my first analysis.

"Wha' time is high tide?" Klinger asked.

"Low was at nine-thirty … so high tide should be about four-thirty?"

"Plee-eeny of water now," Klinger spoke in gentle strokes, perhaps to convince. "Look like it's likely gettin' pretty skinny come ahead. Say we go for it."

The propeller fought to free itself from the bottom marl. I reached for the throttle and pressed the trim, tilting the engine upward, allowing the lower end to breathe. Even with the exhaust exposed and the propeller raised, the skiff continued to lose forward propulsion.

Klinger noticed our problem. "Migh'ave to pole it from'ere awn out, man."

I shrugged, hid my relief, and deadened the engine. "Yeah, this is as far we go. Well, at least we tried, right?"

We sat afloat for a minute. Klinger reached inside his pocket, pulled out the crumpled spliff, lit it, took a healthy pull, blew it out. "Ahhhhhhh."

"Feel better?" I asked. "Why not wait until we get back from this escapade first?"

"Ah, Shamus, we'll be fine. No worries." Then offered, "Need yah a pick me up?"

"More like a pick me *down*," I mumbled.

"Say what?"

"Nothing—maybe when we get back." Then muttered, "*If* we get back."

"Not sure there'll be any lef', man … it's nearly done … get it while yah can."

"I'll take a beer instead."

"Yeah, beer sound good. I'll get me one, too." He finished with the spliff and flicked it into the water.

I retrieved two beers from the cooler and handed him one and kept one, leaned back, and drank a refreshing mouthful.

Klinger was like an energized baitfish. "Gimmie 'at push pole, man."

"You're going to pole us deeper in?"

He gripped the push pole, leading the pointed tip toward the water, said, "Sure, man. It's only another fifty foot."

I peeked up ahead to gauge our route, mumbled, "*Why* the hell not…"

Klinger continued to inch us farther atop the poling platform.

I felt the bottom. "I'm not sure we can go any farther," I said. "The engine's trimmed all the way up and were skimming on chines now." I sighed. "Not sure we've got enough water."

Klinger pointed toward a tiny sandy beach, clear of water and mangroves. "I think w'can cut through right over 'air."

"Can you pole us to it? Looks too shallow to me."

I moved to the bow while Klinger strained. The skiff dug down. "Looks 'bout it, man."

"I'd say so."

We were fifty feet from a porch-sized, mangrove-cleared doorway. Extended branches on either side of the clearing hung heavy, dipping into the water. I opened the front hatch, found a pair of neoprene wading shoes and began to slip them on. Klinger climbed down from the poling platform, listing the boat.

"Got another pair of 'ose?"

I dropped the sun-scorched gym bag where I kept two pairs of boots. "Yeah, in here."

Klinger unloaded the spare wading boots while I checked the front hatch for my emergency rain pants. He held up an ankle, exposing a decent-sized hole of flesh. "What's up wit 'ese holes, man?"

"Yeah, they've been in there a long time, sorry."

I put a pair of khaki rain pants on over black board shorts. I noticed Klinger questioning the integrity of his boots. I grinned. "At least the sole is still intact—should still give you some decent protection."

He stuck his finger into the hole. "Better 'en flip flops, I guess."

In the center console, I pulled out two *Buffs*. A *Buff* is the neck part of a turtleneck shirt, without the shirt part. It's to protect the head and neck from the sun's rays—effective protection against those annoying no-see-ums.

Klinger noticed me putting on the *Buff*. His shoulders dropped. "Aww, man, I to'ally forgot mine. Dang it."

I reached into my pocket, removed the spare, and tossed it at him.

"Thanks, man. Foreskin ... we defini'ely needin' 'ese puppies. Dang no-see-ums'll be killer for sure." He slid the *Buff* over his head, onto his neck, and finished with sprayed bug repellent.

We needed some sort of protection, so I reached into the center console and felt for my Spyderco open-assist pocketknife. Just in case, I slipped it inside a pocket.

My friend straightened his hair, neatened his blue shirt, wiped his shorts, and fixed his *Buff*. "Ready?" he asked.

My reluctance shone like the sun, answered, "Not at all."

"I'm all down for a'venture, man. We sh'go explorin' more often, huh?"

"Let's just hope this stays an exploration mission and not a rescue mission."

Klinger lost his balance clambering off the boat and sank a foot in the mud. My friend's pre-flight check amused me at best, especially when he hit the marl.

"Still feeling lit?" I asked with a smile.

"Maybe so," he replied.

Truth was, I too still felt the influence of the spliff; a little too much for this bizarre situation. Without complete command of my faculties, any misstep could turn deadly.

Klinger sloshed his way to the suspected entry point, hammering at the no-see-ums in the hair exposed part of his visor. I opened the dry box, decided to leave my license and wallet, but pulled out the key, placed it into a pocket and descended from the skiff into the six-inch deep water. I had the anchor and line with me.

The tide was on the incoming, so the skiff should remain buoyant until our return, which, if things went smoothly, shouldn't be long.

And from the storm brewing above, I gazed to its clouds and confirmed a threat was pending.

I paused at the entrance to the mangrove jungle, thinking of all the rumors I'd heard about drug planes using Charlotte County and Shell Creek airstrips for smuggling. Because of their size, those airstrips would be perfect for drug cartels—private and incognito. But dropping drugs from a plane? That seemed a little old-school, juvenile, something conjured up by some never-been-to-the tropics Hollywood screenwriter—and most of all, unlikely.

I reached the creek bank and dug the anchor into the sand, flukes down, and listened to the immediate surroundings. No sound of boat engines or talking. The coast seemed clear.

As if a host showing him to his dinner table, I told Klinger, "After you," and held out my hand.

9

Eliot returned to the wheelhouse and faced Lester. "Whaler lines are nice 'en tight," he said. Lester eyed Eliot. "Good. Have a look toward shore."

The *Itinerant* continued to float off Cape Haze Point. Eliot held the binoculars and scanned toward the southeast, toward Pine Island. *C'mon plane … just get here already.*

A storm had begun to build a half-mile out.

"See anything?" Lester asked.

"No—no sign of 'em yet."

Lester's impatience showed, and he snapped like a sick dog. "Well, look closer, we should be seeing them by now!"

"I'm looking, and all I see is pelicans diving on greenbacks."

"Greenbacks?" barked Lester again, pointing toward the sky. "Up! Look up—in the sky! Not at the damn greenbacks!"

Eliot spoke while watching through the binoculars. "Can't see nothin' but a thunderhead buildin'." He lowered the binoculars. "How are we supposed to see when this plane is comin' with that storm in the way?"

Lester blinked slowly, plucked out a cigarette, and lit it. A vein on his forehead pulsed. He took a drag and exhaled the smoke. "Do me a favor? See if you can figure out the stern bimini for me, okay? If it rains, I don't want the package getting soaked." Lester's register lowered when the smoke hit his vocal cords. "Think you can handle it?"

"Yup … sure thing."

Eliot descended onto the stern deck, stepping to a blue bimini, which was folded alongside the stern gunwale. He scowled and mumbled, "This guy is evil. Straight out of the tight grip of the devil himself. I don't undastand how I got into this. Just do it for the money … do it for the money. I'm sorry, Jesus, I really am. Please forgive me."

After the clasps were undone, as if pulling closed a car's convertible top, Eliot tugged one side of the strap and brought it forward. The bimini went ridged after snapping the webbing into the gunwale clips. Even with the quarter-size holes, it ought to provide adequate protection from the impending thunderstorm.

Lester shouted from the wheelhouse. "There it is!"

Eliot rushed aside. "Where?"

"Right there, see?" Lester pointed high and to the south. "It's right over there. Just came from around that thundercloud—to the right! See?"

Eliot used his hand to block the sun from the sides of his eye sockets. "Oh, yeah," he said. "I see it now."

They both stared at the plane in clear sight through the broken wheelhouse window. It rounded a gurgling thunderhead and flew above Boca Grande Pass, a heading toward Turtle Bay, and a height of one thousand feet.

Lester began moving fast, fidgeting. He motioned toward the stern. "Keep a close eye on it, okay? I'll get the Whaler pulled in. Don't lose sight of it, whatever you do!"

"Will do, will do," replied Eliot and brought the binoculars to his eyes, whispered, "I really hope this doesn't take long and nobody gets hurt. Oh, lord, I've a bad feeling about this. If things get outta hand, I'm leaving. I swear it."

Lester pulled the little boat against the transom and tied it off.

"One push," Eliot muttered. "That's all it would take. Just push this evil man overboard—that'd be done with it. Jesus paid the ultimate price for sinners like myself, to once and for all, wipe evil off this planet."

Lester, gripping the Whaler's rope in his hand, bellowed, "Keep your eyes on that bird. If we lose it, we'll never know where the package lands. Got it?"

"Got it," Eliot said—then muttered to himself, "Who needs to relax now?"

Lester returned to the wheelhouse, seized control of the stationary *Itinerant.*

"Storm's buildin' quick," Eliot said.

"Never mind that storm. You just keep an eye out for the drop. We need to know exactly where it lands."

"Looks like it's gettin' close to droppin' … plane's getting mighty low."

"Where's it at?"

Eliot pointed north, in the direction of Cape Haze Point. "Right over there. See … above those mangroves … see the white limbs? Them dead mangroves?"

Lester's voice crackled. "Okay, I see it. It's real low now … real low. There it is. Okay … okay … there—it's dropped!"

Eliot's eyes focused along the mangrove hedge. "Right above Cape Haze Point, yup."

The package appeared like an ejected fighter pilot. A large box, tailed by a ragged, half-open parachute, dropped behind a wall of mangroves.

"See the parachute?" Lester asked.

"Yup, that's a real good distance back in those mangroves, uh-huh."

Lester became elated. "It's perfect. Perfect spot, don't you agree?"

"Real good … really good."

Lester asked. "See any other boats, do you?"

Using the binoculars, Eliot swept off the coastline, from Cape Haze Point along the western wall of Charlotte Harbor. *Hmmm … looks like Flip's cast nettin' for mullet north of Turtle Bay, right off the bar. Ol' Flip? … he'd net mullet in a hurricane if they were runnin' … no big deal.* Said, "No … none around."

Lester let a deep breath out, relieved. "Gooood, we don't want any interference during the pickup, got it?"

"Surely don't—I mean sure do."

"We don't want to attract any unwanted attention, right?"

Eliot nodded rapidly.

"Good. Now, let's get this package. And remember, after collecting the package, we gotta sit idle for a few hours until the second phone call. That one will let us know the pick-up vehicle has arrived at Ponce de Leon Park, see?"

Eliot patted his left side pocket. "That's right. Got the phone right here."

"The anchor tight?" Lester's tone suggested at test, as though a child having a homework completion check.

Eliot left the wheelhouse and stomped up to the bow to check the anchor again. He focused on where the plane had made the deposit. "That's sure is some thick mangroves," he mumbled. "I've been back there before chasin' mullet. It's very shallow."

The seas were busy, and the harbor water had grown from smooth glass to a light, consistent chop. The boat's list created balance issues as the storm bloomed in the distance.

Lester continued a tight grip on the *Itinerant's* helm, and towards the bar, gauged the tide. A small vibration reverberated when the Whaler bumped the stern.

"The wind sure may blow us out a bit," Eliot noted through the bow window.

Lester ignored him. "Anchor good?"

Eliot balanced from the bow. "Yup. About two foot right here."

Lester replied through the broken window in the wheelhouse, "That's good enough for us. Anchor got a good bite?"

"Good as it's gonna get," Eliot answered, noting the visible anchor through the clear water. After confirming it lock, Eliot climbed off the bow and met Lester astern.

The teak door creaked as Lester opened the berth. "I'll get a tarp from the cabin, just in case. I don't want any issues with this delivery." He went in.

Eliot moved his hands to the front of his body, folding them across his chest like a servant. "Anything you need me to load in the Whaler?"

Lester stood inside the cabin. "You just sit tight!" He began to rummage through boxes, opening small cabinets talking to himself. "Where is that *dog-gone* tarp? I know I got one somewhere…"

"Need me to look up here?"

Lester's tone amped up. "I told you to just wait there … it's here somewhere. I'll find it."

"Okay, just trying to help is all."

"You can help me by checking in the wheelhouse, okay? Wait! I've got it." Lester emerged from the cabin carrying a blue, plastic, square-folded tarp. He pushed it into Eliot's chest. "Here, take this and load it in the Whaler." He stepped neurotically up to the wheelhouse.

Each wave bumped the Whaler into the *Itinerant*. Eliot leaned over the transom and pulled the little boat close enough to climb in. The tarp he stuck under a plywood seat.

In preparation for the small boat ride, Lester checked his pockets. After they seemed clear, he swiped the Zippo from the console and removed the keys from the ignition. He tripped over a fallen bag of junk, hobbled out the wheelhouse, and climbed down to the stern where he met Eliot.

"Ready?" he asked.

Eliot stood in the Whaler while the waves lifted. "Sure am." His brute strength held the small boat against the *Itinerant's* stern, and he waited for Lester to board, but he'd returned into the wheelhouse and began to recheck his pockets. Finally, Lester climbed down from the wheelhouse and into the cabin again. He held two seized, rusted fishing rods.

"What're those for?" Eliot asked.

Lester spoke as a 1930's gangster, "Just in case we run into the fuzz, for cover, see?"

This guy's nuts, Eliot thought.

Lester handed Eliot the rods and then captured one last look toward the *Itinerant* before climbing into the Whaler. When Lester stepped on the small boat's bow, his weight drew it down flush with the water's surface. He faced Eliot. "You drive," he ordered.

Eliot sat, squeezed the primer bulb, kept one hand on the tiller, and pulled a button that opened the choke on the twenty-five horsepower Evinrude. After yanking its pull cord, the engine gasped to life. He put the engine in gear, and the boat puttered forward. Shallow water made no trouble for the small boat's draft.

In the direction of Turtle Bay, Eliot glanced at the fast-building thunderstorm that hovered like a gray halo. He said, "Should have brought us some raincoats."

"If it makes you feel any better, there's a spare poncho in the dry box, next to that red gas tank." Lester spun his head halfway to speak. "It's there if we need them, okay? Better? You're a seasoned mullet fisherman, aren't you accustomed to these filthy afternoon thunderstorms by now, huh?"

A gust of wind hailed across the Whaler and blew off Lester's hat, only saved by the strap under his chin. He straightened it onto his salt-and-pepper-colored head and planted a hand to keep it tight.

The bench seat flexed to its max each time the boat porpoised. Eliot's eyes moved toward Lester's side-pocket. The gun he had flashed earlier protruded, outlined.

Eliot questioned if he even carried the thing loaded, reached and felt for his own weapon, said, "Looks like it should be easy as pie to beach it right over at Cape Haze Point. Then we wade in from there..."

Lester stood, legs spaced for balance, studying toward Cape Haze Point. "Too risky. We should motor in fine from the inside mangrove hedges, I think. I'm not riskin' anyone seeing us loading the package from the harborside."

"But it's a Tuesday. Won't be many people out today, uh-huh."

"I know it's a Tuesday, you fool! I want no issues or problems. Understand?" He acted as if he'd slipped up when calling Eliot a fool. His tone became gentle after he blinked and drew in air. "Now head over toward Turtle Bay—we're getting to it from the inside, got it?"

Eliot nodded rapidly. "Yes, yes. I got it." He pulled back on the engine tiller, and the boat changed course, heading westerly. They rounded the mangrove point at Cape Haze Peninsula and within twenty yards ahead of the small boat, a high-speed flats boat zipped around the corner splattering water, its bow spreading worrisome wake.

"You moron!" hollered Lester, raising his hands in disgust as they approached head-on.

Eliot shook his head in amusement.

Lester's arms flailed in a furious rage. The two men in the flats boat noticed. They began to intentionally stare when the two boats passed port-to-port.

The driver of the flats boat gave Lester the finger and a smile. An oncoming roller hit the Whaler, listing the little boat, close to a devastating capsize. Eliot smiled at Lester's flailing arms.

After the episode, Lester said, "Can you believe those inconsiderate yahoos?"

Eliot replied, "Yeah … yup. Not very nice at all, nope," but thought, *You's the yahoo.*

"Not very busy, you say? Those idiots could have swamped this little boat and then the whole mission would be a complete disaster! I've got a lot ridin' on finding that package. This could be the beginning of many pickups. I need to build trust with these people, get it? And if you follow my instructions, you could be a part of it too … plenty of money. You'd be able to buy a lot of things with the kind of coin we could make. Would you like that, huh?"

Not at all—and I won't be a part of it again. Trying to sound believable but hinting sarcasm, Eliot answered, "Sure, that sounds real nice."

They closed in on the mouth of Turtle Bay. Eliot brought the small boat off plane, and back to an idle.

Lester twisted his head. "What are you doing? Keep going."

Eliot pointed to the sign ahead. "We've hit a no wake zone—see the sign?"

"Oh, for Christ's sakes."

How come he didn't know that? He must not be from around here. Everyone knows of the Turtle Bay idle zone. Becoming suspicious, Eliot said, "Yup—been there for a very long time now. Wouldn't need to draw any unwanted attention, now would we?"

Lester jabbed back. "That's right. You're catching on, aren't you? Good job."

Eliot continued operating the skiff forward at idle speed through the NO WAKE ZONE. weight:

There was the looming storm, and he found himself thinking of his wife and kids—wondering if they'd be all right should anything happen to him. He carried no life insurance, no 401(k), no profit-sharing plan. He lived paycheck to paycheck. His wife, on disability, brought in a meager five hundred twenty-five dollars a month—just enough to cover her medications. Nine years ago, she'd been diagnosed with multiple sclerosis, and now her body no longer moved the way it once did.

Their two kids were in high school, clinging to hopes of college. Debt mounted daily. He'd stopped opening the bills long ago; they simply joined a pile on the kitchen table labeled in his mind: **Not Paid.** Never, not once, had he imagined he'd wind up like this.

Eliot moved one hand to the cross he wore below his neck on a thin silver chain. *Jesus, I don't even know what this package is. Seems to be ... illegal. Why would someone make a drop in the middle of nowhere if it's legal?* He thought he heard a voice, and instincts raised the cross to his mouth where he kissed it.

10

I followed Klinger and marched through a mangrove doorway and into the dense, well-shaded, humid overgrowth. To utilize distance as an effective navigational tool was impossible, and visibility diminished to a bushy ten feet.

Klinger's excitement brought him to the verge of exploding. "This crazy, huh? We're findin' treasure. I'm *sure* of it."

Swiping mangrove leaves from my face, I said, "There's no treasure. It's likely a huge misunderstanding, and as soon as we find this object or whatever it is, it will all be cleared up."

"Don't yah hope it's 'least somethin' interestin'?"

"Like what, a big pile of money, or better yet, a tarp-wrapped dead body? Something like that?"

"Yeah, yeah," replied Klinger, trailing off, sounding though he'd just realized finding a dead body might be a realistic scenario.

We climbed, ducked, and stumbled over branches. I breathed deep, rethinking the agreement with Klinger. I'd very much regret if something were to happen, which positioned Klinger in any type of danger. As the captain of my boat, licensed or not, it was my responsibility to protect *all* passengers and keep them out of harm's way. Klinger has a family, a wife, and a herd of kids. His family would suffer greatly without him. But then, on the other hand, if someone at the drop did need our help, wouldn't it *also* be my responsibility to help them too?

As I stepped over a large stack of dead mangroves, Klinger glanced at my leg, pointed. "Shamus! Don't move!"

"Huh?"

He whispered, "Snake!" Then pointed. "Right by yah leg, man."

I immediately recognized the species. A foot from my left leg, a water moccasin was spinning itself into a wound-tight coil. It spiraled atop a dry piece of mangrove shoot and settled in attack position. Water moccasins, otherwise known as cottonmouths, are extremely dangerous and when threatened, don't retreat. They stand-their-ground and strike when cornered. These snakes hold venom and deliver a painful bite that destroys tissue, but to cause death was rare. This was a snake I wished to hell I had avoided.

"Okay, okay," I whispered. "Don't move. I got this. I'll distract it with a branch." I glanced his way. "Break me off a mangrove branch, okay?"

Klinger cracked a grin. "Ya'know, man … it's illegal to cut mangroves, right?"

I whispered, "Just do it, please!"

Klinger maneuvered in short, pliant steps, dodging debris, and then broke off a three-foot mangrove limb.

"Easy." I focused on the viper's hard-lined, triangle-shaped head and chubby black body, like a brown, sand-filled sock.

Klinger handed my right hand the branch. I held it fingers splayed, palm down, distracting the snake.

Klinger stood steady. "What yah gonna do, Shamus?"

I didn't answer, but to gain the snake's attention, I wiggled the branch astutely across its face. In defense, it coiled up, opened its jaw, and showed us a white, mealy mouth—evidence of an imminent strike. My legs remained sturdy as I brought the branch across the face of the snake, claiming its interest. The snake moved its head and followed the stick. It no longer faced my direction and violently struck the branch.

"Did you see that?" I asked.

"Watch out, man," Klinger said. "Don't need 'at thing bitin' yah, I'm serious."

"What do you think? I'm playing with it or something?" I waved the stick at the snake's face. "I'm distracting it—look."

Now that I'd gotten its attention, I continued befuddling it and managed to swindle away a step, to put distance between us. The snake struck again, and this time it snagged its sharp, hollow fangs, deep into bark of the branch.

"Klinger, look," I whispered.

Klinger lifted to his toes from behind a clump of green-leaved limbs. "She stuck, Shamus!"

"I know." I had to jab my friend. "What are you doing behind those mangroves?"

"Protection, man. Safety first."

The snake stuck deep onto the branch, winding tight, tail squirming like a worm.

"What yah gonna do with it?" Klinger asked.

I rested it between two swollen, hearty mangrove roots, pinned and immobilized.

"You gonna leave it like 'at?" Klinger's respect for nature was admirable.

"Problem?"

He scratched his head. "Nothin,' man. It'll prolly stay like 'at, and event'ally die."

"At least I know where it is, right? Less chance of getting bit by that guy on the way back, huh?"

Klinger answered. "I guess…"

"The snake will be fine. On the way back, I'll make sure it's free, cool?" I scampered back on the chosen path and gave Klinger the thumbs up—he led.

****

As expected, the no-see-ums increased in ferociousness, attacking where they could—nose, mouth, ears. Each exposed piece of skin was susceptible.

Klinger swatted furiously at the bugs on the top of his head. "Dang thin's."

Glad I didn't have that problem—my longer than normal hair provided protection. I brought the *Buff* over my face, covering my nose and ears. The visor I straightened, ran fingers through my hair to remove the leaves and bugs.

Even as the storm brewed, temperatures climbed, and each step claimed double the energy. A cooling breeze didn't exist when buried deep in heavily compacted mangroves, and rendered my shirt soaked through, sticking as though a magnet on a fridge.

We'd journeyed thirty yards through an aerobic-inducing thicket, which took a considerable amount of time. The ground became a bit more solid, allowing us to bear our weight. It had gone from a one-foot-deep swamp to a soggy, supple, sandy floor. After each step, my wading shoes created powerful suction. Up ahead, Klinger waved at me.

"Shamus," he whispered.

"What?"

He was on one knee, pointing down at something. "Look'it this, man," he said, caressing the distinct outline of what might be a hoof print.

I, too, caressed the groves. "Is that a pig print or a deer print?"

Klinger focused on the impression in the dirt. "Oh yeah, man. At'a big boy for sure."

My focus sharpened onto the prints. "Big what?"

"Oh, 'at a pig track for sure, man. See how this hoof's point rounded?"

"I guess … as opposed to what?"

"Look here at 'ese two hoof points. See how 'em are rounded?"

"Yeah…"

"See, deer have veeery sim'lar tracks, but deer a'more pointed than rounded. See how this one is rounded? They walk harder. Yup, no doubt 'bout it, man. Big ol' fat wild hog, right 'ere."

"Great…" I glanced about. "Let's go find whatever dropped and then get the hell out of here."

"Sure thing, man, but let's come awn back here sometime, do a little huntin'. Wha'yah say? Next time I'll bring m'twelve gauge."

"I'm not sure. Can you legally hunt here?"

Klinger answered but sounded unconvinced. "Ahhh … I'm sure it's fine, man," he said, then seemed to rethink, knowing my law-abiding nature. "Me and m'dad did it. No worries. I'll find it out."

Klinger's excitement spiked his Gator accent to the next level. "Hey, now look'ere, there's tracks all over this place." He walked like a leaf caught in an upward gust, blown randomly, distracted by excitement, fingers pointed at the dirt. "Look like a whole dang fam'ly. Let's follow 'em, huh?"

"I think we're getting sidetracked here," I said to inject a sense of urgency. "Let's keep heading toward whatever it is we're looking for, okay? You never know, we might see a few on the way."

Klinger stepped his scrawny leg over the hoof prints and plotted along the makeshift path. Our walking became easier, and the mangroves thinned. As we went on, I saw hoof tracks scattered in all directions, along with an abundance of hog root. I knew salt hogs populated these mangroves but had never expected to see so many signs—not so soon, at least. I reached in my pocket instinctively, pulling out the Spyderco knife, and opened it. Spyderco knives were sharpened to a fifteen-degree angle, making them sharp to a ridiculous degree. If one of these bastards came charging around a bush, I wanted to be ready.

Klinger noticed. "Since ya'got 'at knife, man, how 'bout you take the lead?"

"You'll be fine. Just keep a close eye out … in case we walk up on one of these crazy, testosterone-driven boars."

We continued inching our way to the suspected drop zone. Klinger walked ahead, choosing the not-so-easiest route. The now sunless sky, through the mangrove tips, revealed an anvil of thunderstorm built above our heads. Storms in South Florida build faster than a fire-ant hill after a July downpour, leaving little time to prepare—and it seemed over the years they've gotten worse.

Klinger stopped short, tossed up a closed fist, and cranked his head. "Look over 'air."

I followed where he pointed. A white parachute fifty feet away had gotten stuck high in a dead mangrove tree.

"That's got to be it," I said.

Klinger floundered through the bushes. "Tha's it, man!"

"Wait, wait," I called out.

"It's right 'ere," he said in a hurry. "Let's get awn it, son!"

"Hold on." I tried to snag his arm. "Let's look before we go running recklessly up on this thing. It could be booby-trapped or something. Plus, we might not be the only ones here. Get it?"

"Okay, okay. Less look 'round for a second." Klinger pawed at his face and massaged his thin, short-bearded chin. He slapped a mosquito on his twig-sized legs.

Upon first inspection, whatever fell may not have been a dead body after all. It appeared to be a large crate, how the Arc of the Covenant was packed in *Raiders of the Lost Ark,* but wrapped in tight, black straps. The straps were tangled in the dead mangrove tree, and connected to what I know to be paracord, and then attached to a parachute, which suspended the crate a foot off the ground.

"See 'at, man?"

"Don't touch it!" I said, like scolding a child in a toy store.

Klinger contested, tossing his hands into the air. "Let's cut the dang thing down and check'er out!"

"Hold on a sec!"

"What, why?"

I used ample caution and circled the crate, inching to the opposite side, searching for any clear signs that would put us in jeopardy.

"Dude, let's jus' open'er up already."

I leaned an ear against the crate's surface.

"Are yah seriously lis'enin' to 'at thing, man?"

"Shush for a second."

Klinger stood five feet from me. "You need a ste'oscope, Doc?"

"Funny, but this thing could be a bomb or something, and I just want to make sure it's not ticking before I let *you* open it."

"Hey, why do I'ave to open'er?"

"Because I'm not."

Klinger wobbled back. "Well, I don't wanna open 'at thing by m'self, man."

"Fine, let's go then," I said, turned, and in a meaningful stride, headed back the way we came.

"Okay, okay, hang awn a minute 'ere. Shamus?"

I spun around. "What?"

"C'mon, man," Klinger said, raising his hands. "Let's go ahead and talk this'ing out a minute?"

"Nothing really to talk about. You're opening the box, or we leave, that's it."

He touched his chin in thought. "How 'bout we flip a coin? Yeah, at'ill work, huh?"

I removed my sunglasses, wiped them on my pants. My aggravation crested. "We don't have time to sit here and discuss it. You open it, or we leave, simple. I don't really care what's in it, but I know you do, so—"

Klinger cut me off. "Okay, I'll do it."

Truth was, I did want to know what the crate contained, but Klinger needed to step up to the plate and open it because he'd talked me into this escapade in the first place.

"Okay, let's 'ave a lookie…"

Klinger began his own crate examination, easing to it, sniffing all around it, and stepping warily like a paranoid cat. Next, he glanced at the parachute snagged high in the long-dead tree, and his conclusion was anything but scientific. "W'ale … we'll 'ave to cut this thing down. Tha's for sure, man."

"You need a knife?"

Klinger plucked the paracord, testing its tension. "It's way heavy, man."

I swung the package, same as pushing a child on a playground swing.

Klinger pinched the paracord though a delicate spiderweb, running it through his fingers. "Weighs like a cup'hundred pounds, I'd say. Look how much tension's awn this cord."

"Screw this," I said. "Watch out."

"Ya'gonna cut it?" Klinger now had his hand on the white tree trunk. "We might want try cuttin' the para'ute out of 'is tree first. Just sayin'."

"No time."

Before Klinger could spit out more tobacco, or another word, I sliced through the cord, dropping one side into the damp sand, and then the other.

With the crate on the ground and the parachute cut from it, we could now inspect it for a viable access point. We remained in silence while we searched into the nooks and crannies.

Klinger pointed to a smashed corner. "Look like w'can pry it open from the side, right 'ere."

"Here's my knife."

He snatched it, slid a dirty thumbnail into the slit on the blade's dull side and clicked it open.

The anticipation was sprouting fast, and my intentions weren't to rush him, but time was a factor.

"Go for it," I said.

"Aight, aight."

"Go. Let's do it."

Klinger slid the knife into a small gap between two corners next to a flat-headed nail, bypassing the strapping. He continued prying the two boards apart, separating them enough to wedge his fingers in. "Don't … think … I'can get it with just m'fingers, man."

I handed Klinger a small piece of bark I found on the ground. "Here, put this in."

Klinger wedged the bark into the small gap the knife had created. He pointed to the crevasse. "See if ya'can find m'somethin' to pry this space open with."

I broke a solid branch from a dead nearby mangrove and handed it over. "Anything else, doctor?"

"Dude, this way too big."

"Flip it. Use the other end. We need only enough gap to use more of the wedge; we can slide our fingers far enough in to get some good leverage, then we both yoke on it."

"Yeah, yoke … good call."

Klinger flipped the branch to the smaller end and guided the point to the slight gap created by the wedge and inserted it. As if trying to pry open a manhole cover, he eased the branch down, applying an upward force to the crate's lid. Suddenly, the wood cracked, sending out a screech while a nail pulled loose.

"Air 'it is," he whispered. "It's open now."

"Go for it," I encouraged. "Finish it up."

Klinger readied himself and set his fingers inside the gap. He seemed worried but lifted anyway, stretching the strapping tight while the top panel of the crate bowed but didn't open.

"Need help?"

"Both of us gonna 've to open this, man. It's just bowin' in the middle, look."

"Fine." I slid my fingers into the gap. "You ready?"

"Let's do it," he said.

We slid our hands between the gaps and began applying copious upward pressure.

Klinger paused and raised his nose. "You smell 'at?"

"What?"

"Rain…"

I peeked to the sky and blackness bloomed above. "It's on the way."

He nodded.

"You good?" I asked.

His voice shuddered. "Ready."

"On three, okay?"

Klinger nodded.

"One … two … three!"

Using our combined strength, we drove our fingers upward.

11

After reaching the "Resume Normal Safe Operation" sign, Eliot twisted the tiller drive's shaft, winding up the RPMs, pushing the engine to use every bit of its twenty-five horses to plane out the Whaler. Lester kept a bead toward the area where the aircraft had dropped the package.

The blooming storm had an enthusiastic vibe, like a flower, it wanted to open, to show its full form, all its power and beauty, and would soon provide limited protection from the heat in exchange for soaking rain and lightning.

Lester spoke over the twenty-five-horsepower engine, "Let's hope this storm stays back until we get this package loaded and back to the *Itinerant*. We get in, *and* we get out."

Eliot nodded meagerly.

Traveling north into Turtle Bay, an old fish shack became visible. It was a pleasant site for Lester, and he waved a finger at it. "We may have to take cover in there on the way back ... if we get rain."

"Sure might," Eliot answered. *Does this guy even know that someone owns this fish shack?*

The two continued on, passing the fish shack, crossing to the bay's eastern rim.

As they closed in on the mangroves, Lester waved the finger. "Easy … easy."

Eliot brought the little boat off plane, resting it atop the light chop.

"Down a bit further," Lester said, pointing his stubby finger. "I'm sure we can get to it."

Eliot eyed along the mangroves. "Yeah, yup … that looks like a fine spot."

"I'd say it fell another quarter mile down."

"That does look about right to me, yup."

The boat continued idling parallel along the mangrove peninsula. Eliot had fished the area often and knew it well.

Lester's head swiveled at the fast-appearing creeks, dead mangrove trees, and cuts that ran along the wall of bush. "Which one looks like the best way in?"

"So, there's a real nice'n'skinny inlet right up here," Eliot explained. "Starboard, past this point. I'd say it's the right one. Should work out just fine."

As they neared the mouth of the creek, the engine began to labor, slicing the propeller on bottom.

Eliot peered over the transom. "Real shallow, this one is."

"Then trim the motor up already, would you?"

Eliot released the trim lever, tilting the engine up. They continued for another fifty feet before the propeller could no longer provide thrust and Eliot was forced to shut down the engine. He faced back, looking down at the propeller. "Looks like that's about all she wrote…"

Lester didn't turn, nor look, but rolled his eyes and stood abruptly, causing a portside list. He lost balance in the process and gripped the tiny boat's gunwale. "One of us'll have to push," he said.

"I'd say so, yup," Eliot replied. "Tide's 'bout comin' in pretty quick. On our way out, though, should be plenty water then."

"By the looks of it," Lester said, pointing. "I'd say we have another hundred feet to go, and then around the corner … should be a good place to start."

The boat continued to float idle while Lester surveyed the area, scrutinizing in all directions. He was standing on the bow, hands on hips.

Eliot studied him. His eyes down-casted to Lester's blue-striped shirt, along his waist, where the gun handle protruded from the left overalls' pocket. He sat for an extra minute, waiting for Lester to react.

Lester half-twisted, and it seemed to be mindful of Eliot from his optical periphery.

Eliot waited a few extra purposeful seconds.

Lester took out a smoke, to pass the time.

Eliot breathed deep and said, "I guess I'll hop awn in and push us over."

"Oh, you don't mind?"

"Nope. Nope." *This guy'll have to get in eventually.*

Eliot tucked his camouflage pants into his wading boots and rolled off the gunwale into the water. Behind the engine, he whiffed a mixture of gasoline and oil and began to push the Whaler forward.

At water level, on both sides of the fifty-foot-wide creek, oyster mounds emerged, creating miniature eddies.

He pushed the small boat through the creek and saw Lester grip the gun to make sure it remained snug inside his pocket. *He ain't usin' it, I know it.*

The water, a foot deep, kept Eliot's upper legs dry for now. It would be much easier to pull the boat using the bow line, rather than push it, but he wanted Lester in clear sight. Along the way, he had to dodge full-grown fallen mangrove trees and circular sand holes that lined each switchback. The disappearing sun began to warm his back.

"Ease to starboard a bit," Lester said. "Oyster bed ahead, eleven o'clock."

Eliot moved to the boat's port stern and maneuvered the small skiff, shifting it to the right, which allowed him a restricted view of the water ahead.

Lester stood in silence on the bow, hands on his waist, one foot resting on the raised bow lip.

Eliot pushed the small boat around the fast-approaching bend, and ahead, another turn came into view. He said, "Right here looks like a good a spot as any, yup."

Lester waved off Eliot's idea. "Let's keep going and see what's past the next turn. Might come to find a closer, mangrove-free spot."

Eliot wondered if he hadn't said anything, would Lester have wanted to take the next turn? In fact, Eliot did know a better spot past the bend, since he had often stood in this very creek, holding a cast net, waiting for unsuspecting passing mullet.

Moving along through the creek, thunder echoed off the reflective water—rain was close. When South Florida brinks on the verge of rain, a certain smell develops in the air. A smell of growth, of refreshment, of the possible amnesty from the repulsive afternoon heat—a feared, and also cherished situation.

Approaching the bend, Lester waved at Eliot to stop.

"Everythin' okay?"

"Yes, yes, just give me a second, will you? I thought I heard something—a noise."

"Well, there are plenty of—"

Lester waved his arm behind his back from the bow. "Shhh!"

Eliot pulled at the transom, keeping the boat stationary. Both men listened closely to the ambient noises.

Nothing but the tide dripping from mangrove limbs, rolling down the roots, and the calling song of Blue Jays were audible. Lester was intent on hearing something, or someone. He listened, cupping his ears— trying one ear, and then the other. After he waved the go-ahead, Eliot continued pushing the small boat.

"Everythin' fine?" Eliot asked.

Lester sliced a finger through the air, to his lips. "Shhh!" His neck craned forward, peering past a mangrove tip, to glimpse the absolute first view ahead. He waved his hand to halt the skiff, pointed ahead, mouthing, "Boat."

This complicated things for Eliot. He whispered, "Well, what be our next move?"

"Hang on a second, let me think," Lester muttered. "This is what I didn't want to happen." His hand found the grip of the gun. "One thing's for sure; we must get that package." He hobbled off the bow. "Pull us back a couple feet, out of view, okay?"

Nodding, Eliot reversed the Whaler a few feet until the boat was no longer visible. "What type of boat is it?"

"It looks like that same boat we saw this morning runnin' across the harbor, remember?"

"Sure do, yup."

Now, to both, it was obvious that those two fishermen had indeed seen the plane, and even more likely, the package drop.

Eliot said, "Maybe those two needed to use the restroom or something…?"

Lester raised his brow, unhappy with Eliot's statement. "I'm sure that's *not* what they're doing. There's only one thing to do now…"

"What's that?" asked Eliot.

"We go claim what's ours."

Eliot swallowed. "What happens if they don't want to give up what they found?"

Lester wrapped all his fingers around the butt of the gun. "Oh, they'll give it up one way or another."

Both remained silent for a few minutes. Thunder rumbled with distant growling from the clouds, and the fringe of the storm boiled overhead, oozing like a run of lava.

Eliot said, "Should we go in another way … or the same way they did?"

"Quiet and let me think."

Eliot gazed at the foreboding, storm-filled sky and thought, *This guy better do nothing hurtful. I bet that gun ain't even loaded.* He felt the outline of the knife. Standing in a foot of water next to the Whaler, with a hand on the gunwale, he trudged forward through the suction-like sand and strove for an easy peek around the bend.

"Don't let them see you!"

Eliot stopped in his tracks and retreated.

Lester spoke in a whisper. "Don't make any noise, got it? We don't want to lose the element of surprise."

"Yeah—yup."

Lester pressed his hat atop short, silver hair. "Okay, this is what we're going to do. We anchor here. What is the depth … two-foot max?" He faced down to Eliot, who stood in an inconsistent one, two feet of water.

"That's right … 'bout one, two foot, yes."

Lester clacked his teeth in thought. "Okay, we start here. The Whaler's out of view, so we sneak over to the skiff and investigate. Maybe we get the registration numbers off the side, and then we gather any info we can about these two. Got it?"

"You mean like their wallets and what-not?"

"Yes, anything we can find that would be useful to us."

Lester pulled his boots up tight, tucking in the leg-bottom slack of the overalls. He stepped to the gunwale, sat on his butt and lowered into the water. The bow scraped his back as it shot up.

Eliot sloshed to the bow, lifted the anchor, and dropped it into the water. The anchor chain rattled off the bow lip rub rail and then muffled while the fluke dug in.

"Ready?" Lester asked.

"Yup, sure am."

Both men began the short wade to the mysterious skiff. Lester's grasp tightened on the pistol's grip in clear view of Eliot's eyes. They used caution approaching the skiff, which sat floating in a foot of water. Both men paused five feet from it.

Eliot focused through the bushes and along the creek. "I don't see anybody 'round."

"You just keep a close eye out. Any noise at all, you let me know, got it?"

"Yup, uh-huh."

Lester waded near the skiff and noted the registration numbers on a sticker across the bow. Next, he shifted toward the front hatch and opened it. Inside were a fire extinguisher and emergency toolbox.

Eliot admired the skiff. *That sure is one beautiful lookin' boat.*

Next, Lester stepped over to the raised console and opened the compartment beneath the gauges. From inside, he retrieved a translucent, hand-sized dry box and pulled out a wallet. Casting a quick glance around to make sure no one was watching, he flipped it open.

Inside was nothing but a license and twenty-seven dollars in cash. The license read: **Shamus Pickford.**

Lester pocketed the cash and the license, then slipped the now-lighter wallet back into the box. After returning the box to the console, Lester waded back to Eliot.

Eliot continued a worried lookout, mumbled, "I really hope those two fishermen cooperate and don't do nothin' stupid."

Lester arrived. "Okay, I found a license from a fella named Shamus. It has his name and address."

"What you need that for?" Eliot said.

Lester's eyebrows slanted, lips pursed, a crack of a smile appeared at the corner of his mouth. "In case these two don't want to give up the prize, I'll have an ace up my sleeve," he said, using the license as a pointer. "C'mon, you need to be learnin' from me if you want to eventually become partners, see?"

Eliot kept his expression flat. "What now?"

"We go get what we came for."

12

Klinger and I attempted three more times to remove the crate's lid, but without a hammer or pry bar, it couldn't be done, at least not by us. Someone had sealed it well, as though it would survive a drop from a plane.

"Well," I said. "There you go."

Klinger leaned back, scratching his head. "Nails really in tight, huh?"

"That's the truth. Need a hammer … or saw."

"Now, hang awn, man." Klinger stepped to the nearest white mangrove tree and began shaking a rather large limb. His whole body hung like a playful monkey.

"What are you doing?"

"See, I figure w'can smash it. Use this tree limb and smash the dang thing open."

I took a long breath and had to give my friend credit. Under different circumstances, it would have been a decent option, but at the moment, it didn't fit with my plans.

I said, "I'm not so sure that's what we want to do. I don't think it would be wise to *smash* into it. Prying okay, but smashing? Not so much…"

Klinger sensed my reluctance and turned up the tree-shaking intensity. "Oh, we'll b'fine. Put'a little faith in your ol' pal, huh?"

The whole tree began to shake, hinting to snap at any moment.

"Aaany minute now, she'll give in … jus' gotta keep at it, see?"

"I see that." An uneasy vibe gave me pause. I listened. Why would somebody drop a crate from a plane in the middle of nowhere?

"Almost 'air." My friend now used all one-hundred-and-fifty-pounds on the branch, causing small cracks to spew out plumes of nature dust.

"I don't think it'll break," I finally said.

"Sure it will, man. No reason it won't. Just gotta stay at it, like the wind from a'urricane." His legs swung back and forth, increasing the gravitational force, careless as to the repercussions.

"Hurricane, gotcha. Listen, I'm going to take a piss while you do your thing there. But if it isn't broken by the time I get back, then we leave."

He began straining. "Take ya'time then. I'll get'er down."

"Seriously?" I cringed at Klinger's dedication but knew my friend well.

"Oh, yeah … 'ese limbs? Break all'a time, trust me."

"I'll be back in a minute. And try keeping an eye out. Then we get the hell out of here, cool?"

"Yeah, man. Ten-four."

I left Klinger and tip-toed through the mangroves, searching for a reasonable spot to piss. After a few steps, I heard a crack, like split wood, and then a soft yelp. I laughed inside.

Moving along, I caught the sound of a far-off engine. A whine emerged from the harbor side of the peninsula. Cape Haze Point was, at its bulkiest, a quarter mile wide, and the package had landed in the middle. After the piss, I heard the boat again.

The harbor side had to be nearby. I didn't realize I'd walked as far as I did. This side of the peninsula was less dense than the first half Klinger and I had forged through earlier. I went on and came across additional dead-standing mangrove trees, wider game trails, and much, much more hog remnants, including root.

I reached the harbor and became shrouded in no-see-ums.

Above, the thunderstorm poised to tease and merge, to engulf the entire peninsula—classic Florida. I marveled at its size, panned to the water level, searching for the source of the outboard I had heard. About two hundred yards out, I laid eyes on a mullet boat spot-sighting fish—the source. Only one man I knew brave enough to be out in such inclement weather, on purpose, was Flip, my neighbor.

I peered through the mangrove branches after swatting away the bugs. Flip hadn't the visibility to see me, so I didn't wave. I checked my phone—no signal. A rumble of thunder echoed. After facing up to the storm and breathing in deep, I was now eager to return to fishing, so I fast-paced back to Klinger.

13

Lester and Eliot studied all areas viable for the best point of entry.

"Where would you suppose they went in at?" Eliot asked.

"Well, there looks like a good spot about fifty-foot across, near that dead mangrove tree, see? It seems like a decent place to enter, and the only clear spot anywhere around."

Eliot studied the area in question; an internal battle to stay positive lingered. "Oh, yes ... that could be a very nice place indeed," he replied. "Might even be near the package, yup."

"Let's go, and for the love of God, be quiet. Can you do that?"

"Yup, sure can," answered Eliot.

Before leaving, Lester waded alongside the gunwale suspiciously. He arrived at the stern of the vacant skiff and fished a razor knife from his pocket, opened it, and his meaty hand began slicing at something toward the bilge.

Eliot didn't like what he saw. "What's that for?" he asked.

"Insurance," replied Lester. "Now c'mon, let's go."

Highly flammable fuel surged into the flats boat's bilge.

"Was that necessary?" Eliot asked.

"Look, do you want these two messing up our plans? I sure as hell don't! If we go take the package and they cooperate without any problems, then we'll help them fix it, okay? Sound good?"

"I suppose…" Eliot replied. *He's crossing a line. Damaging another man's boat?*

Lester led the way toward the bank. Eliot towered behind, gliding his feet through the sandy bottom, stepping where Lester stepped.

Lester's next stride was careless, sloppy, and he paid for it, sinking his right leg up to his thigh.

"Sh—"

"Everythin' okay?"

"Yes, everything's fine!" Lester snapped in a whisper. "Let's just keep going!"

The two men reached the small clearing and noticed the mud held a clue. Lester knelt. "You see this?"

"Are those—?"

"Yes, yes, shoe prints. Fresh ones, too."

"I see, yup. Sure are. Look real fresh."

"Two sets," Lester added.

Eliot pointed his chin. "They must be close. Right through 'em mangroves."

Lester said, "Gooood, you're getting it."

"Not too hard."

"Okay, let's go get this package. I'll lead."

"Fine by me."

Lester brushed ahead and into the mangroves. Eliot ducked under and followed.

In the bush, Lester climbed over knobby roots and had to stoop under the branches, at times struggling due to his weight. He filled his lungs numerous times.

Eliot worked his way methodically through the bush, picking routes to avoid overexerting himself.

Lester's gun, after each step, almost slid from his pocket, which the swamp would consume. He asked, "Didn't look as thick from the water?"

Eliot swatted branches from his face. "Nope, sure didn't."

Lester remained still, and after a short ponder, focused straight ahead. "I'm pretty sure this is the route they went," he said, pointing to the entwined roots of a mangrove tree. "See the muddy shoe prints down on the roots here? See the gray mud?"

"Oh—yup, sure do." Eliot peeked, where a broken mangrove branch was snapped to a sharp point, it's center still moist and dense with nutrients that had been sucked up from the saltwater, then filtered; it was smeared in gray-brown mud and Eliot confirmed to himself that the men had walked this path.

Lester flinched and froze in place. After a long step, Eliot caught up.

"Everythin' okay?" Eliot asked.

"No, it's not! There's an ugly son of a bitch snake in the way!"

Eliot had himself a look. "Just a moccasin…"

"Just a moccasin?" Lester slipped out the gun and aim up a shot.

"Wait, now." Eliot stepped ahead. "Let me just move him along." He did just that after learning the snake had wrapped itself tightly around a branch. "No need to shoot, nope. Element of surprise, remember?"

Lester rolled his eyes, said, "This way..."

Both men continued trekking along the narrow path, dodging small swamp puddles. The ground began hardening, and soon, the earth morphed into damp, salty sand.

Lester stopped and knelt. "Look what we've found here..."

Eliot could see the clear outline of two sets of shoeprints. "Yup, there they is."

Lester shifted to another set of tracks. "Oh, and would you look at this?"

"Yup, those are some hog prints, uh-huh."

"Looks like the shoe prints go this way." Lester waved. "C'mon."

They followed the tracks in silence, stepping carefully on the intruders' unmistakable prints. Eliot's large foot flattened the shallower impressions left by the fishermen. From behind, he stood a full foot taller than Lester, easily seeing over his shoulder and beyond.

When Lester crouched, Eliot mimicked.

Lester pointed off to his left, into the bush. "There it is."

In a tree, up twenty feet, hung a white parachute. Eliot followed the parachute down to its cord. In mid-swing with a large branch, one of the two fishermen they had spotted earlier began a backswing, then hammered down onto the wooden crate.

Eliot faced Lester and nodded. *Please cooperate.* "We just wait 'til they leave, right?"

Lester conveyed the point in a peeved whisper. "Hell no! That package belongs to us. Look! He's smashing at it with a damn tree branch! We're going to take it!"

"Okay, okay. What kind of plan you got?"

A soft whack of wood on wood echoed in the distance.

"Well," Lester said. "Where's the other one? Weren't there two aboard? Looks like the driver's missing. Do you see him?"

Eliot bent low and peered through bushes and trees but saw no other man. "Don't know, can't see much from here, nope."

Lester gawked at the unwelcomed intruder. His mouth drooped open, constructing his next game plan. "We've got to hurry," he growled. "It's about to start pouring rain. Follow my lead, okay? I'll talk to him. *You* watch out for the other one, got it?"

Hyper-aware, both men trundled off the beaten path and crept toward the crate. Eliot searched for the other man. Lester concentrated on the trespasser.

Moments later, they encroached on the personal space of the unsuspecting fisherman. The intruder was focused entirely on the crate, didn't see nor hear the two men closing in. Before he could slam another whack, company arrived.

"How's it goin', buddy?" Lester asked the man.

Startled, the man convulsed like a child caught with a lighter—voice high and fragile. "Uhh … what's up?"

Lester spoke to him like he was a toddler, curious about his toy. "Whatcha got there?"

Reaction came from attempting to hide his wrong doings. "Ahhhh—not sure—jus' um … found it walkin' t'take a piss."

Lester stood feet from the man, raising his chin. "Oh, did you now?"

"Sure did."

Lester pulled his gun out and knocked it on the crate. "You didn't happen to see this crate fall from a plane, did you?"

The fisherman eyed the gun. "Uhh—plane? No, no, didn't see no plane, man."

"Right…"

Eliot recognized the man. They'd passed each other often living in the same town but couldn't name him. He decided to make a stand. "You said no one was to get hurt."

Lester ambled to his side, hard and swift. "Will you shut up!" he said in his face—then whispered closer to his ear. "Just scaring him is all, see?"

Something the unknown man held behind his back filched Lester's attention, used the gun as a pointer. "Everything okay … something wrong with your hands?"

"Uhh … Nope, all's good," the man said.

"Well, then, let's see them."

The man brought empty hands abreast—looked past and saw Eliot. Seemed he recognized him, too.

"Are you trying to be funny, son? Do I look stupid to you?"

"No, not a'all." His attention snapped back to Eliot.

"Turn around," Lester barked.

The man eased a hand to his backside.

"Turn around, now!"

The man clenched the tree branch, where it had been resting against his shaky shoulder blades.

"What do we have here?"

"Jus' a tree branch is all. They fall from trees all'a time, man."

"Toss it over here, nice and slow, got it? No funny business."

The man hesitated tossing the branch, or weapon, aside for one second too long.

Lester blew away a bug from his lip. "Are you thinking about taking a swing at me, boy?"

"Why would I do 'at?"

"Many reasons. Now, toss it here."

The man did as he was told, and the branch landed near Lester's feet.

"Take it!" Lester said to Eliot.

"Where should I take it?"

"Just hold onto it for now, okay? Can you do that?"

"Can, yup."

Lester's jaw clenched. "Why don't you check on the crate, see if this little maggot damaged it, okay?"

Through intimidation, and fearing Eliot might take a swing at him, the fisherman backed away.

Lester said, "I hope you didn't do any damage now."

"Didn't damage nothin'."

"We'll see…"

Eliot knelt, ran a hand along the corner, the same corner where the man had been hacking. He avoided eye contact. "It's got a small crack, uh-huh, right on the seam."

"Really now?" Lester hobbled to it, leaned in, and inspected; eyes widened. "Seems a few nails have come loose, too."

"That was 'air," the man said defensively.

"Oh, was it now?"

"Sure was."

"I highly doubt that."

The man said, "Fell from a'plane. What sup'ose to happen to it?"

Lester had one hand on the crate's cracked edge and spoke to Eliot. "See if you can tighten this back down."

"Uh-huh."

Lester asked the man, "So, are you gonna tell me where your friend went to?"

"Friend? I ain't got no friend."

"You're telling me that you didn't hike back here with a friend? About six feet tall, wearing tan pants and a white shirt?"

"I don't know what yah talkin' 'bout."

"Boy, do you know what kind of trouble you're fixin' to be in?"

The man filled his lungs, swallowed hard, and straightened his spine to appear formidable.

Lester said, "I'm only asking you one more time. Where's your friend?"

The man shifted his stance and caught Lester's eyes. "What friend, man? It's only me 'ere."

Shaking his head, Lester pulled out the ace. "Okay, fine." He held up the license. Through the mangroves, he shouted, "Shamus Pickford, from Punta Gorda, Florida. I know you're out there. Either you come out now, or your little friend is goin' get hurt. Understand?"

The three men remained still, in silence, listening for a response. All that sounded were bird chatter and closing-in thunder.

Eliot began searching for a suitable device to hammer back the nails. He remembered the knife in his pocket, decided Lester didn't need to know he possessed it. Using the dead branch, he haphazardly hammered the seam back in place.

"Will you shut up!" Lester snapped, walked laboriously to the crate. He eyed the brush line one more time for the absent fisherman. "Eliot..." He faced the unknown man, returned to Eliot. "You take this end." The fisherman froze when he pointed the gun in his face. "And *you* take *this* end."

Eliot and the man began a one-hundred-and-fifty-yard hike back to the Whaler, carrying the package as though a man on a stretcher.

After a final glimpse for the missing fisherman, Lester conceded and followed in line.

14

Through mangroves, I discovered further-mounting hog tracks while roaming the not-so-obvious path back to the crate. I hadn't detected as many tracks the first time through. It appeared a large team had stopped to root here, then high-tailed it back into the bush.

I didn't waste another second pondering the possibility of an encounter with a wild boar and resumed hiking toward the crate, and it was better for the both of us if he'd gotten nowhere near inside of it. This fiasco needed no more of my time, and rain was soon to fall. I hit the trail and sped off.

I set a good pace, but my motivation to get back to fishing came to an abrupt halt, like a blunt knock on the head after hearing the voice shout: "Turn around!"

I crouched and listened. The shouting sounded as though it came from the crate's direction. Klinger! My heart began to thump in my ears, teetering on the verge of a chest-bursting explosion.

In a crouch, I crept toward the voice, cataloging every sound that rose with each careful step. My body tensed. Through the scant visibility, I slipped behind a rotting mangrove and peered out, managing a low, imperfect glimpse of the crate, Klinger, and the two men.

I recognized the man standing feet from Klinger—it was one of the men from the *Itinerant* we saw earlier.

A short, silver-haired, pudgy man wearing a bucket-style hat and holding a gun, stood next to my friend. The other stood close to the crate, inspecting the corners. He was much taller, at least six-foot-four, bulging shoulder points, and tight, tan skin. It was Eliot Waldrup, Flip's dear friend.

I heard more talking I couldn't quite understand, and from a modest vantage point, glanced again. Confusion set in. Why would Eliot have himself involved in this? My thoughts began a racket inside my head.

The obese man holding the gun spoke to Klinger, shouting: Shamus Pickford, from Punta Gorda, Florida. I know you're out there. Either you come out now, or your little friend is goin' get hurt. Understand?"

Standing in shock, I didn't reply, but stood stunned. How did this guy know my name and where I lived? Did he somehow squeeze it from Klinger? No, I knew Klinger to be solid as a rock. He wouldn't tell him anything.

In the man's hand appeared a card. It hit me: my wallet. They must have traveled in from the same way Klinger and I had, so my skiff was easy to spot. They obviously saw the crate drop, same as Klinger and me, and decided to investigate—or more likely, and obvious, they were waiting for it.

The short, podgy man used the gun to give orders. Klinger and Eliot lifted the crate as though it would explode and began to carry it back toward the beach.

Fast assailing panic swept over my entire body. All other emotional positions would suffice right now, but not panic. I tried to control my breathing, slowing it. After I managed two deep breaths, I thought my options through. It appeared the gunman was too weak or too obese to carry such a large crate. It was also plausible he only needed Klinger's help transporting it. After that, the most probable scenario: maybe he lets Klinger remain at the skiff, where I could meet him? Or this one I didn't like: shoots Klinger after no longer needing his help.

There happened to be a long-dead mangrove tree where I could wait anxiously, which allowed them enough time to gain space. I decided to follow them at a safe, undetectable distance. After a tense five minutes, I stalked toward the trail, stopping at the drop zone.

There, I searched for anything that might help identify the short man with the gun. He had left nothing behind but the white parachute, which hung like a treetop teepee.

A lightning bolt pulsed a blinding flash, followed by a thunderous rumble. No way to sidestep it, the storm was here, and there was nothing I could do about it.

Before leaving the drop site, I thought in regret of my friend. I *knew* we should have skipped the investigation—should have gone back to the house, cracked a couple of beers, and do what we always do after a fishing trip: reminisce over the fish we caught and debate over different ways to cook them. Instead, I'd led us into danger. The guy had a gun for Christ's sake! What if he shoots Klinger, or Eliot? What if he kills them? I'd never be able to forgive myself.

I became dizzy, pressed palms to my ears, pressurizing my head. I struggled to listen—heard light chatter in the distance. I ran.

On the move, I rounded a short bend in the trail and nearly stumbled into a fallen tree blocking the path. I was feeling good, making decent time, when a wild pig burst from the humid, green underbrush, three squealing piglets on its heels. My spine locked; muscles seized tight. The sow was massive—easily two hundred pounds—and stood just twenty feet away.

As the pig's sight veered, it saw me and went rigid. Instinctively, she cut off the angle to her piglets, swinging her milk-filled mammary. My heart raced, almost to the point of passing out. Fear had frozen me. Panic again. My fight or flight reflex kicked in and I spun eyeballs only, searching for the safest route to escape. I gazed into the eyes of the salt hog. She'd made her mind up—protect her progeny or die trying.

An attempt to evade the animal was also not an option. They had the advantages in these mangroves, and I could *not* outrun it, or fight it. No problem, I have a knife. I reached fast for it, but it was missing. Klinger! He never gave it back!

I suddenly spotted what might be the *only* option—a half-fallen mangrove tree leaning against a thick bundle of dead stumps. The tenuous log rested on discarded debris and began two feet off the ground and angled upward like a playground slide. If I could run up, without getting gored, it might give me a chance, or at the very least, create a diversion and distract the animal, enough so to slip away.

My eyes returned to the sow; its long brown snout sniffed upward, wet nostrils flared, huffing in human scent. The beast appeared to be missing its left bottom tusk that had probably been lost in a fight. It had thin, light brown fur and a flaxen tint; eyes black, evil, hatred-filled; its head down, ears stout at attention. The animal wanted me gored to death, and it would if I made a single step forward.

I spoke to it like if talking to a rabid dog. "Easy, buddy … *easy* now."

More lightning followed by thunder. Sweeping downpours began.

The pig grunted, a warning signal that I'd run out of time, so I fled for the white log.

The pugnacious sow started after me at full speed.

I mustered a final burst of speed and leaped onto the tree just as the wild animal gnawed my thin, fast-soaking pants, ripping a hole at the heel. I shimmied up as though the ground was on fire.

The sow attempted multiple times to follow, but fell short, and slipped down. Sharp hoofs tore off chunks of white, dead bark.

I waved and flailed like a maniac, but it didn't motion to leave. I had to lead it away somehow, so I broke off a branch and tossed it in the opposite direction.

"Get it, girl."

It moved two steps, sniffed at its purpose, but returned.

"Now what?" I mumbled.

I shimmied in the tree, felt an object wedged in my belt. The flare gun! I rushed it out from my belt, brushed small amounts of swamp debris off the orange plastic, and carefully aimed it at the mud-covered pig. After lining down the barrel, to the sow's eyes, I mumbled, "Good luck, buddy."

I decided differently and swung the aim off a headshot, to the side—a shoulder shot. Nanoseconds before pulling the trigger, rain dripped down the bill of my hat into my line of sight. I adjusted and fired.

The cartridge wasn't defective as the date had originally indicated. With luck, it bounced off the hog's shoulder and landed beside it, flashing a bright, red, glimmering flame. The pissed off, now frightened sow, ran off into the bush. The three piglets followed like a shark remora, tight, pressed up to its hairy belly.

Only after the coast seemed clear enough did I maneuver off the log. Even with the rain, the flare flamed strong.

Relieved, I stamped it out like a campfire and covered it with mud.

I carried on after no other thoughts monopolized my attention. After maneuvering tactically over dead trees and ducking again under mangrove bushes, I came within fifty feet of the beach. With non-existent visibility to the beach, catching Klinger would be a miracle. The pig situation had cost me a lot of time.

That's it, I thought. I had to rescue Klinger. I pulled up the *Buff* that covered my face and whispered, "Here goes nothing."

I rushed through the remaining swamp, struggling at times, but to my pleasure, busted through the last bit of brush, somersaulting onto the limited shoreline.

15

Lester shouted at the man, "Hurry up. Pick it up. Quit dropping it."

"Okay, okay … What's big deal anyway?"

"You think I'm stupid, boy? I know exactly what you're doing."

"This thing mus' weigh 'bout two hundred pound."

Lester changed his tone and spoke as though he needed to bargain. "You're a young man—should have no problem carrying it. If you do as you're told, then you won't get hurt. Got it?"

Eliot and the man connected sight. *Do it kid.*

At six-foot-four, and two-hundred and fifty pounds, Eliot carried the crate's bulk in an awkward backwards walk, which made it easier on the other small man, who was a mere buck fifty. They lifted collectively and slid the box over mangrove limbs and dead-rotting fronds. Lester pinned a close eye on both men.

"This thing yours?" the man asked Lester.

"What did you say?"

"I'm jus' askin'… this box yours?"

Lester stepped to the man, exposing yellow cigarette-stained teeth. "You listen to me and listen close … there's no talking, got it?"

"Just wonderin' what all the deal is?"

"Deal?"

"Yeah, what's all in this thin'—?"

"Shut up!" Lester snapped.

Eliot's eyes opened wide. *Don't piss him off, boy. We almost done now.*

They continued walking the final fifty feet in awkward silence. Eliot walked backward but led the way.

Into the final feet before the beach, the man dropped the crate again, but this time he collapsed onto the lid.

"Boy, you better pick it up … and quick. We don't have much time!"

"Time?" The man breathed heavy. "What's 'at mean?"

"Never mind, you!"

"'Bout to rain, yup."

All three reached the end of the mangroves, coming upon the small beach. The tide had returned, and the sandy bank had lost half its size. Blackness hovered overhead.

Lester removed his sweat-stained hat, gazed at the storm. His words were governed, an attempt to hide the frustration while he spoke to Eliot. "We need to keep this box as dry as we can. I want you to go get the Whaler and bring it here, okay? The tide is right where we want it. Plenty of water now."

Eliot began his short wade around the bend to the Whaler. The rain lightened. Once there, he pulled anchor, slung the bow rope over his sweat-soaked shoulder and began hauling the small boat as though it were a satchel of boulders—mumbled, "Damn kid! If he didn't mess things up, I would'a just took this boat and left Lester right where he is and go back to the dock and call the police, yup. Instead, you had to piss him off. Your face is familiar as a roe-filed mullet. Where have I seen you before?

"Jesus, I ask of you this one request: lead me to the answers for I can find?" Realizing the water was deeper than it had been earlier, he decided to use the engine, motoring the short distance to the beach.

Back at the bank, the man asked, "Did yah kidnap 'at guy, too?"

Lester replied, "Now, what's that supposed to mean, *boy*?"

The man cracked a smile. "Jus' curious is all, man. No biggie."

"Do you know what *I'm* curious about?" Lester lifted the gun to his eyes.

The man swallowed hard. "What?"

"I'm curious about the look on your friend's face when he finds your bullet hole-riddled body lying in the mud ... dead."

The man no longer smiled. But instead, scowled at Lester's face, sighting crow's feet cornered eyes, defined by gray, overgrown eyebrows. His nose, short and round, and his doughy neck, discolored from years in the sun, had damaged skin like patches of a fungi-infected lawn.

"So where is your friend anyway? No rescue attempt? Not a very good friend if he just leaves you, huh?"

The fisherman's tone was ominous. "I tol' yah, man, I came 'lone."

Lester shook his head, pointing toward the skiff. "Lie all you want, kid. I saw you two come in on that boat, so enough with the games. Plus, I have his license in case he tries doing anything *stupid.*" He lit a cigarette and conquered a puff.

"Hey, can I 'ave one?"

"Boy, you got to be out of your mind—"

"Jus' askin'..."

Lester took a drag, formed his lips to an oval and blew toward the man's face. The man wrenched his head from the fading smoke ring.

"Speaking of licenses, I'll need yours right about now."

"License? I ain't got one."

"Turn around!"

He did.

"Lift your shirt!"

He showed a scrawny, hairless, rib-lined chest. "Happy?"

"Don't get smart with me, boy."

Lester frisked him like the police, found a wallet, cell phone, a knife, and a can of Copenhagen. "This is a nice knife." He placed the knife and can inside his own pocket and checked the wallet for money. The license, he pinched from the clear plastic slip. "Klinger Lee Nowell."

Klinger stared at the man. "Wha' yah gonna do with that? Come to m'house if I step out'a line?" He snorted.

"You're getting on my last nerve. I have a job to complete, and if you think I'm letting you two screw it up, you're sadly mistaken. Get it?"

"Can't take a'joke?"

Lester's jaw clenched but said nothing.

Both men looked up as the rain began again. Eliot drew their mutual attention while he rounded the mangrove point. The small outboard sputtered, blending in with the light rain.

After Klinger attempted to place Eliot's identity once again, he asked Lester, "Can I 'least 'ave a dip? You know, from one tobacca user t'another?"

"Dip?" Lester said. "You can't be serious."

"C'mon, jus' one pinch? Lemme pack one…"

"If I give it to you, will you shut up?"

"Yes."

Lester's eyes rolled.

"T'anks, I guess."

He handed it to Klinger.

Klinger slipped the can between his middle finger and thumb. His index finger shook and smacked against the lid to compress the tobacco tight, and as if it were his last, packed a full lip.

Lester waited open-handed for Klinger to return the dip, which he did grudgingly. After it disappeared into his overall pocket, he pointed Eliot to the cleared tiny shoreline. "Right here. Bring it over here!"

Eliot left the engine running, slipped into the water, and met the two on the beach.

"Grab this strap," Lester said to Klinger.

Klinger lifted one side of the crate, passing it off to Eliot who then lifted his end and heaved it into the Whaler. After, Klinger peeked at Eliot for some sort of telepathic instructions, trying to place his identity. Eliot kept his head down.

Lester said, "Eliot, grab the tarp and cover this up. It's going downpour again any minute. Aren't you paying the least bit of attention?"

"Yup, sure is." Eliot held the tarp and wiped off the rainwater.

Klinger leaned to offer help in tightening the corners and met Eliot close enough to whisper. "What's all in this thin', man?"

"Just do what he says," Eliot responded.

Eliot peeked and noticed Lester distracted, scoping back to the mangroves.

Klinger saw it too, seized the opportunity and pressed for information. "What's really goin' on, man?"

Eliot remained silent and finished wrapping the crate.

"C'mon, man, what's up with this box?" Klinger raised his voice. "I mean, why was it dropped? What's it all 'bout?"

Eliot exposed protuberant eyes after sliding off his sunglasses. "Look, kid, I don't got nothin' to do with you, but I know you from somewhere, so let's just be nice 'en cooperative and take this package wherever it needs to go—then we go home, okay?"

Lester stomped to the boat. "Shut up, you two! Didn't I say no talking?" He climbed to the bow, dripping black mud deposits across the wooden-planked seat. "Eliot, you're driving back. Boy, you're sitting right next to me … so I can keep an eye on you."

The crate rested on the bow. Lester and Klinger sat behind it, their size using up the entire bench.

Eliot fast-twisted the throttle, and the Whaler sped away from the lone skiff. He smelled fuel. A flash of lighting lit up the sky.

Maneuvering past the now sunken mangrove trunks, Eliot steered through the last switchback before reaching the openness of Turtle Bay's flat water.

Lester spun and spoke to Eliot. "Give me *your* wallet."

Eliot, baffled, removed his gator-skinned wallet that had been given to him as an anniversary gift. He watched it gather rain. "Uh—don't think that's very necess—"

"Give it to me!"

Klinger cocked his head, and watched Eliot submit.

While motoring away from the creek, a storm was full-bore above their heads. Massive thunderheads encompassed the bay and most of Charlotte Harbor. Seas rolled high, and the skiff's flat bottom cuffed into each wave, spraying seawater mist into their faces. The risk of becoming swamped was a real possibility. A sharp gust loosened one corner of the tarp—it began to flap.

Lester leaned forward and adjusted it, re-covering the crate.

It wasn't long before Lester waved Eliot to slow the boat. "God damn rain," he said.

Klinger laughed, facing up as raindrops landed onto his sunglasses. He said, "So, where we goin'?"

"That's none of your concern," Lester answered.

Klinger swiveled his head at Eliot who controlled the tiller from behind. "Not sure this lil' Whaler gonna get us too far."

Eliot lifted a silencing index finger to his pressed-shut lips.

Wide-open Turtle Bay lay ahead, while a darkening wall of storm swept steadily in their direction. They plowed onward, circling aimlessly, waiting on Lester's guidance to continue. Round after round, they gained no ground, just water churning under their hull.

Eliot twisted the throttle, and the small boat pushed along, laboring to lift on plane. Lester glanced back to Eliot, insinuating fault that the little boat was hundreds of pounds over the maximum load capacity. The skiff surfed the waves, and after a slow, arduous plane-out, Eliot aimed the boat toward the wall of rain. All three men braced for a wet ride.

A lightning bolt snapped the water shortly after they entered the rainstorm, followed by a violent crack of thunder. Eliot charged the small boat toward the location where the lightning had struck.

The next strike appeared to have set Lester uneasy. Eager for cover, they emerged through the mist. Lester pointed toward the old Turtle Bay fish shack.

Eliot ignored Lester and didn't deviate from his course, kept charging straight toward the dangerous storm.

Klinger noticed the subordinate reaction from Eliot.

Lester, after failing to get his way the first time, pointed aggressively toward the fish shack. "GO, GO, GO!" he wailed.

Eliot forced the tiller away from his body—a hard starboard bank, aiming the boat straight toward the old fish shack.

As the men pulled up to it, the rain pushed down like an over-bearing water massage.

"Grab that rope," Lester said to Klinger.

Klinger resisted, a rebellious jab, maybe an attempt at finding a weak spot in Lester's stroppy authority.

Lester only smirked, took the rope from Klinger's hands, and stepped to the bow. His weight, plus the crate, lowered the tiny bow deck to water level.

The fish shack sat well above the water—even at high tide. So, to avoid crashing into a pylon, Eliot flipped the twenty-five-horse engine into reverse and braked the skiff, docking within inches of the piling.

"What we doin' 'ere?" asked Klinger.

"Do *you* like getting rained on?" Lester answered in a rush. "I sure as hell don't. We're riding the storm out in here, whether you like it or not."

Lester moored the small boat to the dock three-and-a-half feet above the bow. He somehow managed himself onto a plank like a toddler climbing onto a couch. "Get that crate up here, pronto!" He waddled up the steps to the shack's door.

Another nearby thunder rumble echoed, this time juddering the hardwood dock. Eliot shook the tarp puddles that had accumulated, removed the tarp, and found that the crate had remained dry. They began lifting it onto the waterlogged dock.

In the pouring rain, Klinger leaned into Eliot. "Quick … let's take this boat and motor the hell out'a 'ere!"

Eliot didn't respond.

Rain provided cover from his voice, Klinger added, "Man, c'mon, now's our chance. W'can leave his ass *right now* on the dock 'en escape!"

I would love just to leave both these guys behind, Eliot thought sadly to himself, *but that's not what God has planned for me. Plus, I've made it this far, and I can't quit now.* "Look, kid," he said. "I can't leave, okay? I need the money we're bein' paid for this real bad, got it? Real bad. Plus, he's got our wallets, so…"

Suddenly, a deafening high-pitched echo swept down from the shack after a loud, shock-silencing BANG percussion hit Eliot and Klinger.

Lester stomped down the dock steps. "Get that crate up here, immediately!" he said, aiming the gun at both men.

Eliot and Klinger lifted, jerked, and yanked the crate onto the dock, and up the steps to the main deck. They hurried to approach the door where the combination lock had been shot to pieces. The black spinner knob gone, leaving an inward-shot hole.

Lester held the door open as Eliot and Klinger brought in the crate. To all three men, the sound of rain hammering the tin roof became disruptive and soothing at the same time.

16

I f it weren't for my skiff floating atop a rain-boiling creek, the beach would have been empty. The wind had blown the boat arbitrarily against mangroves. They had taken Klinger.

Trying to stave off panic, I drew a deep breath, filling my lungs. It was imperative, now more than ever, to summon only the clearest thoughts—unclouded by emotion, stripped of sentiment. Those were the thoughts I chased. They were crucial in facilitating a reasonable plan. So far, that method had proved impossible. How should I get him back? Could I follow in the skiff? Call the cops? I will *not* rat. Never going to happen. That crate was important, an obvious fact, and its value appeared higher than *our* measly little lives. Following them in the skiff might work, but as soon as I faced the exposure of open water, I'd be seen easily from a mile away. Suppose they did spot me, then what? They'd just give Klinger back?

Why would they take Klinger anyway? He was not involved in any of this. Did he mouth off? Knowing Klinger, that was a real possibility but kidnapping him? And what's Eliot's involvement in this? I've known him to be a docile, gentle man, who wouldn't hurt a fly.

Something was off. I had a strong inclination about where they were taking him, though. They must have used the Whaler's narrow draft to motor into the treacherous oyster-laden shallows, and I remembered they'd moored it to a certain twenty-four-foot Stamas. Obviously, they were headed back to it, but then where? Could I intercept them in time? I had to think of something fast.

After a short, unfertile ponder, my top course of action was to follow, so I waded to the skiff, where a rainbow-colored slick fanned out beside the stern. A strong stench of fuel vapor clung to the inside of my nose.

I flinched as lightning flashed, snapping down thunder. My jaw clenched as I climbed aboard and stepped astern, where the overwhelming odor nearly choked me. Then, a shocker: the entire bilge was filled with fuel.

Fuel no longer firmed up the primer bulb. I traced the hose back to the engine and found the problem—they'd sliced my fuel line clean in two. Whoever did this was up to something serious, and it was clear Klinger was in grave danger because of it.

I ripped open the front hatch and removed a box containing spare parts, hoping to find a fuel line coupling. I found a spare bilge pump, ten-amp fuses, a few feet of fourteen-gauge tinned marine wire, and some electrical tape, but nothing practical to repair the severed fuel hose. At times, I had also kept spare parts in the center console, so it was worth checking. After I shuffled through the chaotic mess, inspecting things that might work to repair the line, I stuffed the flare gun back into the rear hatch.

I sat impatiently in the captain's chair and realized the one thing left to do was push pole my way out. But that would take time—time I didn't have—time Klinger didn't have.

I reached for the anchor, now submerged beneath the steady push of the incoming tide. Then it struck me—Flip! If he was still on the other side of the peninsula, he might be my only shot. I checked my phone for a signal. Nothing.

I wasted no time, put the phone away, dropped the anchor back into the mud, leaped into the water, charged through the mangroves, heading back to the harbor side of the Cape Haze Peninsula. The first couple of steps in were dry before a heavy round of downpours hit, an instantaneous soaking.

I continued at a fast pace, striving to remember the best route from the previous trips. The crate had well-defined the trail after it had been drug through. Ducking and climbing over and through the thick bush, I realized throwing in the occasional jog might be wise.

I continued trekking sleuth-like to the opposite wing of the peninsula. I rounded a brief break in the mangroves, stopped, listened, and observed. Doing so slowed me, but I had to check for wild salt hogs. Another standoff wasn't what I needed—or wanted.

I reached the end of the mangroves, noticing the tide had risen to worrying heights. Suddenly, a branch cracked behind me. Pointing at me from twenty feet away, a spiked-tusked salt hog breathed rapidly, head lowered.

I froze.

It sniffed the air.

"Unbelievable," I mumbled. There was no time to waste, and sort of doubtful this thing would swim after me, so I made a break and slogged overtop the last mangrove limb into the harbor water, thrashing clear of the evergreen hedges.

Due to the rain, and the darkness the thunderstorm shed, visibility dimmed to a meager hundred yards—the violent storm overhead hovered at near-full strength.

I cast a glance north toward Cape Haze Point, hoping to spot Flip where I'd seen him earlier, but the water lay empty. I searched along the northern mangrove wall, still nothing. He must have headed home for shelter. Flip never minded fishing through most storms, but the raw fury of this one might have chased even him off the water.

I decided to check south, ahead of a small mangrove outcrop a hundred yards away. I began to wade through the corrugated, white-capped, waist deep slow-going water. I forced on, trudging along even though waves crested into my chest.

Exhausted, I reached the outcrop. Seconds before giving up, I detected a lone mullet boat tucked into the mangroves—one that sought shelter.

Flip had wedged the nineteen-foot boat into a finger creek underneath an abandoned osprey nest, a first-rate cover spot. His thin body was swimming in a pair of bright, banana-colored fishing waders.

With arms flailing, I waded toward him using all the willpower I could rally.

Flip stood from his stern seat, set down a soaked magazine, lowered his neck and squinted—he saw me.

"Flip!" I shouted through the rain, laboriously thrashing through waist-deep water. I reached the boat dog-tired. Flip saw me from the bow.

"Shamus … that you?"

I rested hands on the gunwale. "Klin—Klinger's been taken."

"Taken? Whatcha mean?" He extended his hand. "Here, getcha self up awn in here."

Taking his hand was like gripping an iron claw coated in liquid sandpaper. The connection flashed confusion into my thoughts. How Flip would react to his long-time friend as a kidnapper, I hadn't a clue.

He pulled me aboard, and I collapsed atop a pile of dead mullet. It took a few moments to catch a breath. I moved underneath the T-top to escape the rain.

Flip spoke in slow pulses, "Take it easy. Now, what's this talk 'boutcha friend?"

"Did you see a plane a while ago, the one that was flying insanely low?"

He nodded delicately. "Uh-huh, sure did. Nearly went down … thought

'bout checkin' it out." He glanced out to the harbor. "But this rain…"

"Well," I continued. "We saw it drop some sort of box … went to investigate. At the drop zone, two men came and took Klinger. They loaded the crate, forcing him to go with them." I breathed deep.

"Oh, really … that's no good at all." He pulled in thought, down at his beard.

"I went to piss, and when I came back, I spotted the two men screwing with Klinger." Flip had a right to know that it was his friend Eliot, but I wasn't yet ready to let that info known. I continued, "One of them has a gun! But they didn't see me hiding behind a dead mangrove, though. And they ransacked my skiff and stole my wallet. They know where I live!"

Flip realized the seriousness, said, "That's amazin', Shamus. Well, why didn't yah take the skiff and get to 'em?"

"That's the thing; they cut the fuel line!"

Shaking his head, "Awe, son. That's an awful thing to do, just awful. What ya'gonna do?"

"Oh! And I also nearly got eaten by a wild hog and her three piglets."

"Piglets, you say?"

"Yes, they pinned me in a tree; almost got me on the way out."

Flip's face twisted into a confused grin. "Oh, really now?"

"Yeah, I used a flare gun to distract it."

"Well, well, not surprising." He pointed. "I'd seen plenty up here 'round the bend there, crossing the creek. So, what yah to do?"

"I'm not sure, but I know one thing, I've got to get Klinger back, and I might need your help."

"Why not call awn the cops?"

"I can't get a signal through this storm, and I'm soaked. My phone's probably shot. Besides, calling the cops would be a disaster, given the look of those two. I'm no rat. And who knows who really owns that crate? I'd rather it just get to wherever it's headed."

Flip eyed his console. "M'radio's broke too…"

"Yeah, I don't even carry one."

Flip turned toward the open harbor. "What's awn the inside of this crate?"

"That's the thing, couldn't open it."

"No, huh?"

"We cracked a seam … but couldn't quite see its contents."

"That's really strange, Shamus. Wish I had answers f'yah."

I hobbled up and turned toward the sandbar. "I know where they're taking Klinger. I mean, I'm pretty sure I know."

"Where's that?"

I explained to Flip while he stood at the helm, fingers clamped, wrapping the black composite steering wheel. "To an old Stamas cabin cruiser … anchored a few hundred yards off the bar. In tow is a small Whaler. I'm sure they used it to motor back into the shallows, and probably heading back *as we speak*. It's not far from here, maybe a mile or so." I pointed at the massive storm. "Right … about … there."

He glanced out. "Well, Shamus, that's not s'far."

"No, it's not. Only thing is, it's dead straight through the heart of the thunderstorm."

"If your friend needs our help," he said. "Then let's get awn to it."

Flip unclamped his hand and cranked the engine. He said from the wheel, "Grab that push pole, Shamus, and push the stern out a hair, woul' yah?"

I spiked it straight through the water, deep mud, and flexed it out like an Olympic pole vaulter, sending the bulky stern off from the mangroves.

Flip put the nineteen-foot Sheffield in gear. The boat idled out toward the inside bar.

Visibility was improving enough, but hard rain still fell.

As we headed south, Flip said, "Le'me know when ya'think we should cross."

"I'd say any chance you have, you go for it."

Flip hammered the binnacle, lifting the boat. It settled on plane quicker than any boat I had ever ridden in.

Raindrops pelted my skin like the sting from thousands of mosquitos so I relocated under the T-top, where Flip stood at the helm.

Using little effort, Flip's boat sliced through the never-ending, white-capped harbor. I pointed toward where I thought the *Itinerant* should be.

"You got a game plan, Shamus?" he asked in a raspy voice.

"Not at all," I answered.

Flip smirked.

We approached Cape Haze Point and a boat appeared—the *Itinerant*. I waved Flip off plane, and he pulled off the throttle.

Flip said, "That looks like your boat right awn over there."

"Sure does," I replied.

We sat idle one hundred yards off the *Itinerant* while I tried summoning a fresh start to a new plan, an effective plan. "Let's get a bit closer," I said.

Flip eased the boat ahead.

The small boat was missing. "Where is it?" I muttered. "Did it even make it back? Did it sink? Since Eliot and the short man made off with Klinger, even at idle speeds, they would've had plenty of time to return. Maybe they weren't on their way back?"

Flip heard me. "Anything's possible," he said, and inched near the *Itinerant*. "W'ale, does that look like your boat?"

"Oh, yeah, that's the one alright. No doubt about it."

"Small boat missin', huh?"

"Yeah, they should have been back by now, I'm sure of it." I stepped to the bow, focusing closer. "Looks like no one's home."

"Sure don't," Flip replied.

"Hey, pull around to the bow for me? I want to check the registration numbers, just in case."

Flip circled the boat.

"Do you have anything to write with?"

"Hang awn. Let me check the dry box." Flip opened a weathered green cooler and came up holding a small pad and a bowling pencil. "Here you go."

"I'll just read them to you, okay?"

"Mmm-k, ready." Flip tested the pencil on the paper, drawing a small circle.

I said, "Okay, FL 0-1-2. Let me see here … looks like the last two are … um … I can't read it. With the chop, I'll never see it."

Flip engaged the engine to reverse. "Well, we got most it anyhow."

"Let's just hope we don't need it."

We bobbed a couple of minutes next to the *Itinerant*.

I said, "Hey, do me a favor? Throw that fender out for me? I'm boarding it."

"Board it? Well … al-right then." Flip motored the mullet boat closer, but the three-foot, inconsistent waves made it impossible to lash.

I suggested, "See if you can try coming up from astern? I'll climb on the bow and jump off."

Flip reversed the boat, turned, and backed off. He re-routed the bow and circled back, pointing to the stern of the *Itinerant*.

I climbed to the bow deck and dropped to a crouched position. The three-foot waves threw off my timing.

"Steady," I told Flip.

The boat bobbed up and down as if it was a mechanical bull. Crouching tight on the dip, I timed the up lift and sprang onto the *Itinerant*.

My timing was off, and I landed feet short of remaining above water. Armpits slammed into the transom and my sunglasses flew off and skidded across the stern deck. I lifted a left leg over the transom, heaved aboard the boat to a crunch landing. A weathered, blue bimini top with quarter-sized holes dripped drops of cold rainwater while I sprawled on my back. I stretched for the sunglasses.

"You all right, Shamus?" Flip called out.

"Yeah, I'm fine." I stood up, working a shoulder kink—noticed a smile forming on Flip's face. "You like that?"

"Aww, c'mon now. You'll be a-okay."

I scanned the boat, and its hideous condition where there were broken windows, brown rot smears on the deck, and deep rust stains surrounding each corner, every bolt. Cracked fiberglass along the gunwales had been poorly patched, showing lumpy resin bubbles.

I ascended to the *Itinerant's* wheelhouse. There appeared to be no working instruments, and an old CB radio dangled from the ceiling—its power wires ripped bare, exposing thin copper strands. Glass from broken windows crunched under my feet. Ashtrays, cigarette butts, and empty match books filled the instrument dash.

A small compartment under the steering wheel looked odd. I leaned and checked the contents. Inside, nothing of significance but a few empty boxes of .22 caliber gun shells and a roll of sixty-pound repair leader. No registration paperwork or insurance information. I checked through the broken windows for any signs of the returning Whaler—none.

I jumped down to the stern deck, and found the small cabin. Inside, a detectable eye-watering fungus kind of smell stung my eyes. I had a pretty good idea what it could be. A boat this old and neglected? Black mold. I protected my face using the *Buff*.

A rogue wave caused an abrupt list to the boat. I lost balance, falling forward onto the red cushions lining the cabin's birth. Clothes on hangers lay on the sheet-bare bed. I decided it would take a month to search it then a strong vibe of revenge clouded my thoughts. I felt the urge to disable the vessel as mine had been. Eye for an eye… Street justice applies to the water, too. I glanced around for an easy reach retribution, but became the wiser and exited from the cabin. I motioned Flip to swing closer and pick me up.

Flip idled the mullet boat as close as he could, but I climbed over the stern gunwale anyway and dipped in the water. Wasn't risking injury by leaping again, and since I was already soaked, I might as well swim to Flip.

"Stay there. I'll come to you!" I shouted from the water.

My first thought after I left the stern of the *Itinerant* was hoping Flip did not pinch me between the two boats, but he appeared to maintain a safe distance.

In my pocket, my phone swayed in the salty current.

I tried to figure how things went so horribly wrong. Several hours ago, Klinger and I had been sitting in the backcountry enjoying the beautiful weather, catching fish, and catching a buzz. Things were going well, and now, a man I considered a friend, had kidnapped another friend? I breathed deep, let the thought go.

I reached the stern of Flip's boat, having done my best not to drown, and heaved over the gunwale, falling on a familiar pile of crisp, dead mullet.

17

The scent of fresh cut wood overwhelmed the interior of the fish shack. Walls were bare—only studs and plywood separated them from the elements. Three sets of bunks pressed against each wall, totaling six beds, shaped like a U. Two green, folded Army blankets sat at the foot of the sheet-less, pillow-less mattresses. About forty square feet in total size and had an A-frame sturdy corrugated tin roof. Gray outdoor carpet covered most of the wooden floor. A makeshift sink ran no water, just an exposed PVC drain running along the floor. Next to the sink, a propane-fueled camping stove sat underneath a petite, pressed-wood cabinet. Above the bunk beds, a small TV/DVD combo sat near the ceiling on a corner-filled shelf, and on top of it, a pile of assorted DVDs.

Klinger and Eliot slid the crate to a space near the sink.

Lester said, "You two sit on the bunks." He showed his back and made for the painted white cupboards that bolted ahead from the front door.

Eliot and Klinger sat across from one another. Both watched in contempt as Lester snooped, opening doors, rummaging through drawers, making a mess. Canned food, plates, a wad of napkins half-filled the shelves.

"Wha'yah lookin' for?" Klinger asked.

"You never mind that, boy."

Lester reached behind the door, to a narrow storage shelf. He closed the door just enough, squeezing a lawn chair out from behind it. Its legs upon spreading created friction, screeching the rusted hinge bolts. On the threshold, he sat half inside, half out, eradicating their chances of escape.

The small shift in Lester's weight, polyester bands crackled and popped, stretching to their maximum load. He lit a smoke and pulled hard, loud, leaned back, and peeked on Klinger and Eliot. Eliot dropped back as if to take a nap.

Klinger spoke to Eliot using his eyes first—then widened them and nudged his chin toward the door, waited a few seconds, and whispered, "W'need to take the crazy son'bitch out."

Eliot used an index finger to lower his sunglasses. His eyebrows were slanted. He nodded toward Lester and shaped his hand to a gun. *This guy won't give up. He better just settle awn down and let us get this package to where it needs to go. He better just watch it, or he'll get us both killed.*

The black grip of Lester's gun protruded from his white overalls' pocket.

The gritty rain shower outside the fish shack pounded against the tin roof. Downpours came in hammering, intimidating waves, sweeping across the tin, before yielding to a light drizzle, and repeat. Lightning sent Lester curtly to his feet.

"What'a matter?" asked a cocky, smirking Klinger. "Lightnin' too much for yah?"

Lester sighed. He moved to the cupboards and opened the doors, fumbling for something. He placed an old beef stew can onto the counter next to the sink and sifted like a gruff child through an opened drawer of silverware. After coming across a fork, he found a metal can opener with a corroded cutter wheel. Not bothered by the orange corrosion, he opened the can, used the fork, and gave it a taste. Satisfied that the meal wouldn't kill him, he wobbled back to the chair, managing a seat. He began to shovel it in.

Klinger asked Eliot, "Ask if I'can have a can, man— please?"

Eliot shook his head. "Ask your own self."

Lester finished the can of stew and set it on the threshold beside him and dropped the fork into it. His pocket contained a much-wanted pack of cigarettes and a Zippo lighter. He went for it and lit another smoke, pulled hard at the filter and announced the outward breath with a satisfying sigh.

Klinger's elbows rested on his knees, chin in his hands, staring at Eliot's frosty, stoic expression. He whispered to him, "What all this for, man?" Klinger now rocked his leg, heel-tapping the floor. "Can yah at least tell me 'at? … I mean—a crate in the mill'of nowhere?"

Eliot leaned forward, peeking for clearance to speak. Lester sat staring out at Turtle Bay, attention outward toward the water.

Eliot whispered, "Why do you need to know anyways, huh? I'd think that a man in your position would think that the less he knows then the better off he'd be!"

"So … Yah *do* know where it's goin'?" Klinger pressed.

Eliot revisited his previous position, leaning back, arms crossed.

Lester rocked out of the chair and hobbled into the house, dropping the empty can of beef stew into the sink, fork and all. He pulled out a bottle of water with a faded label on a shelve behind the door and twisted off the cap. He chugged the whole bottle in three loud, refreshing gulps. Then crushed the bottle and tossed it into the sink.

"Can I 'ave a water, man?"

Lester faced the men, paused, sighed, found two more bottles, and tossed one at Eliot and another at Klinger, who let his fall on the floor. Klinger retrieved the bottle and both men cracked off the caps and began to drink.

Klinger finished his water. "AHH," he directed at the gunman.

Lester returned to his seat watching the harbor, wearing a complacent smile. Intrusive water now filled the Whaler, and he seemed to decide it had to be drained before it over-filled and slowed him down. He mumbled, "Well, if you're not ahead of the game, then you might as well not even be in the game. I know just who's draining this boat, and it *ain't* me."

He stood from his chair and stepped into the shack again. It was clear his mind looked for a bucket, or a large container for bailing. A manual bilge pump tucked away in the corner behind the door caught his attention. He handled it and pointed a finger at Klinger.

"Here, take this," he said.

"What yah want me t'do with this thing?" Klinger replied, receiving the pump and examining it.

"Don't you know what *that* is?"

"Um, yeah, man, 'course I do."

Lester faced toward the doorjamb, went to it, and pointed down to the small boat. "Well … get to it."

"Get'ta what?"

"You take your ass out there and drain that boat … *before* it sinks!"

"But it's pourin' rain out."

Lester leaned in closer, pressing forward with intimidating force. "I don't care if there's a tornado out there. Get down and drain that boat!"

Klinger petitioned Eliot's support but got none. At the roof's eave, he paused in a dry spot and gazed overhead, toward the black mass dumping down large, painful drops. He was no stranger to afternoon thunderstorms, but this was a spine-tingler. A few hours ago, a nice rainstorm would have been a welcome and refreshing break from the afternoon heat. But staying soaked could lower his body temperature to dangerous levels—warm water hypothermia it is called—and it can kill.

He shivered walking along the dock, down the steps to the flooding boat. The pump Lester forced on him wasn't the most efficient device. Sitting on the driver's bench seat, he morosely lowered the suction end into the rainwater next to the battery, and the drain hose went over the lip of the transom. The device resembled a manual bicycle pump—the bottom of the pump acting as a suction point and the air hose as the drain.

The only other way to drain the water out was to run the boat on plane and pull the drain plug, let gravity and momentum draw out the water through the plug holes.

He began pulling upward on the pump's handle, sucking water up through the cylinder. After pressing down, it shot it out the drain and into the bay.

The rain pulsed onto his back and shoulders, and a steady wind howled across his face.

Klinger knew Lester watched his every move. He muttered, "Prolly worried I'm gonna make a run for it, or better yet—swim for it."

"There you go. Just like that!" Lester shouted from his chair, twenty feet away.

Klinger ignored him and continued the repetitious transfer of water. After each pump, it seemed like the storm rained half of it back into the Whaler, but he kept on.

Lester gazed out toward the eastern side of the bay, noticed a faraway boat. Klinger eyed it as well.

Lester rested his hand on the grip of his gun. "You don't worry about that boat now … keep on pumping. Storm ain't over yet. Need it good and dry."

Klinger became more defiant, smiled fake-like, shook his head, and mumbled, "Jackass." He gazed out toward the east. "'At boat look a lot like Shamus's friend, Flip's. Maybe he'll find Shamus and figure a way ta'get m'ass out 'ere."

18

After landing hard into the boat, for a few seconds, I remained flat, catching a much-needed breath. I reached for my pocket after standing and removed my soaked phone. The screen was blank.

An exploding echo of whistling fragments streamed across the water, but from a considerable distance away. I turned and moon-eyed Flip. "Did you hear that?"

Flip had already crouched. "Sure did."

"Gunshot?"

"Sounded like one to me…" He then added more concern to his voice. "Off in the distance, and it ain't duck huntin' season."

"No, no it's not."

Flip stood with caution. "How far would yah say it was?"

I stepped to the bow. "Not sure. You know how sound travels over water … it echoes pretty good."

"Sure do … f'miles."

I faced Turtle Bay Inlet, a quarter mile away. Small surges of incremental adrenaline spurted into my spine. I began an anxiety-riddled rant. "Would this guy really shoot Klinger? He tends to be a bit lippy, but shoot him?

This is crazy, what if something happens to him. What if?" Then I thought, *Eliot?*

Flip's eyes were wide. "That's pretty serious stuff, now."

"Let's head over to the mouth of Turtle Bay, but let's take the cut that runs along the mangroves. Just in case we see them on the way, I'd rather be close, near shore. I doubt this goon even knows about it. If you're not from around here, which I'm sure he isn't, you'll be the wiser sticking to the channels."

"Sounds right by me," Flip replied, levering the nineteen-foot Sheffield into gear, and we began the short trip to the mouth of Turtle Bay.

I added over the engine, "Whatever's in that crate is probably illegal. Whoever's expecting this thing wouldn't be very happy if the shipment didn't make it to wherever it needed to go—safe and intact."

"I see'er point."

"I'm just worried that since they haven't come through Turtle Bay Inlet yet, that something serious has just happened." I cleared my throat and raised it above the engine noise. "They've had plenty of time to make it back to that *Itinerant* ... unless they detoured or something."

"Storm's a lookin' pretty bad right now," Flip said. "Heaviest rain is now right awn over Tur'le Bay, right where we're goin'... maybe they went for cover?"

"You might be right. And it means only one place they would've gone to seek shelter, and that's the old fish shack on the northwest bank of Turtle Bay."

Flipp nodded. "Know that shack well…"

"There're other shacks out there, but the one in Turtle Bay is on their way. They'd have to motor right by it. And with the rain, it makes perfect sense."

Flip said, "What do ya'suppose we do from here awn out? They'd see us as soon as we hit the mouth enterin' Tur'le Bay … no cover."

"Correct, we'd be fully exposed," I said. "The rain could provide some cover, though, but it falls unpredictable."

We approached the NO WAKE ZONE as we entered the channel leading into Turtle Bay. Flip throttled back and lowered the Sheffield back near idle speed.

So we were, after a quick glance, indeed the only ones around. South Florida storms weren't for the weary. It wasn't surprising we hadn't seen another boat.

Flip eased the throttle back to neutral, and we bobbed for a few moments. Then I slipped to the bow and signaled with two fingers. Flip nudged us ahead a few feet. I wanted the earliest possible glimpse of the fish shack before we cleared the last mangrove outcrop. We crept forward, stealthy as fish shadows, and when we finally slipped past the final tangle of green, the old fish shack emerged—looming and ominous.

It appeared to have occupants. A clear outline of a small boat was visible, but too great a distance to get an exact identification.

After hand-motioning to Flip, he reversed us from sight. I huddled under the T-top to escape the rain.

"There's definitely someone there. I see a small boat. Might be them, might not—it's hard to sight through all the rain."

Flip made a rapid movement toward the rear hatch. "Grab awn the wheel f'a sec."

I straightened out the bulky Sheffield—lining it parallel with the mangroves. No more than ten feet away, Flip rustled through extra equipment and spare parts and appeared holding a pair of binoculars.

"Here, try these," he said.

I looked them over.

"I keep 'em for scopin' mullet. I reckon they been in here for a few years now. Forgot they was even on the boat."

Against my eye sockets, dust and mullet juice covered the lens for horrible visibility. "You got—"

Flip handed me a dry, torn rag. I wiped off the lenses and the eyepieces, looked again. "Much better, thanks."

Flip took the cue and bumped us forward beyond the mangrove tip. Visibility became adequate. Using binoculars to find something a half mile away wasn't an easy task. I found a starting point near the southern side of the fish shack and focused on the far-off mangroves. I scanned and kept level along those mangroves until the house came into view. A quick index-finger focus adjustment and there they were.

"I see them."

"Yeah?" Flip asked.

"Yup, that's the small boat."

I hunkered back under the T-top and returned the binoculars to Flip.

Flip was now reversing the boat out of view. "See Klinger?"

"Sure did, and you're not going to believe what he's doing."

"Oh, yeah? What that'd be?"

"He's standing on the dock holding a manual bilge pump."

Flip opened his mouth with amazement. "Is he—?"

"Yup. He's forcing Klinger to drain the small boat's bilge, I bet you."

Flip molded his white beard and pulled it down, tugging down a frown. "So, you don't say…"

"That's what it looks like to me. Can you think of any other reason he'd be holding it?"

"W'ale, I suppose not, no. Any sign of the other feller?"

"He must be inside. The big question is: How we're going to motor over unseen? The fat ass knows who I am having stolen my license."

Flip lowered his voice. "W'ale, he don't know who I am, now do he?"

"No, he doesn't. As far as I know. So maybe…"

"Are you suggestin' that I get out of my boat and wait here while you go'n check it out—recon?"

I studied the mullet. "That's one option, I suppose. Or we could do this. I lay down here." I pointed to the pile of mullet in the gunwale.

"Awn the mullet?"

"Yes, right down here below the gunwale," I explained. "And you drive by the shack. Try to get the best view *you* can, but not *too* close that Klinger will recognize you."

"Okay, I see."

"Once you pass the house, keep going, there'll be a small curve a few hundred yards beyond the fish shack, to the north. Should provide enough cover to stop without getting detected. It would be a good spot for figuring out our next step."

Flip shook his head and said, "Ready when you are."

"Let's go."

Flip put the mullet boat in gear and noticed something odd, and pulled it out

of gear. The engine bogged hard. He peeked over the edge, using the steering wheel for balance.

"I'd say we're caught up—prop's bitin'. We'd gone and drifted a'bit too close to the mangroves and up awn a small branch. Foot's hittin' pretty good."

"Alright, hang on." I jumped into the water, waded to the stern, and rocked the boat free from the branch. I hopped back aboard. "Let's get to it."

Flip resumed idle speed.

Seconds before we reached the last point before exposure, I dropped to my knees, positioning under the gunwale overtop a pile of slime-coated mullet.

"Comfy?" Flip smiled.

"Funny—let's just go already. Remember, just keep going, even if they wave at you, okay?"

"Got it," he said and hit the throttle. The boat lifted off, rolling a cluster of mullet from Flip's productive day toward me.

Flip didn't throttle down until reaching cruise speed at thirty-five miles per hour. We hit a rough patch of chop, and my head slapped into the belly of a long-dead mullet, coating my face in a thin layer of funky slime. At that very moment, I thought about many other places I would rather be than this shapeless mission. One thought stood above most, one that brought me closer to a woman who I'd been spending more and more time with, scraping boats, Sara Albright. As my lustful thoughts increased, maybe nestled between the sheets, a combination of body heat, fueled from a striking conversation, among other things… Flip broadsided another white cap, spanking a slick mullet against my face, and the dream was gone. Hard rain took its place.

According to his gaze, I knew we were lined up. The fish shack was west of us, so Flip's examination should be accurate. I watched as he tracked the shack in passing.

He continued for a few hundred yards, bringing us to the point we'd discussed earlier. Flip pulled the throttle back once again, and the boat settled on its own wake. He motioned "all clear," and I stood.

"What did you see?" I asked.

"It was real hard seein' anything, but it look like a round man's standin' out awn the deck, under the eave. Maybe the same feller that was askin' around Frank's last week. Could tell right away he wasn't from 'round here.

Your friend's down in the Whaler pumpin' out rainwater. No doubt 'bout it, alright."

I grabbed my chin. "Interesting … so you know the guy?"

"W'ale, I don't know him, know him. I overheard 'em lookin' 'round f'some help, side work kinda stuff when I was in there sellin' m'mullet last week. He said he was a mullet fisherman, but *I've* never seen him b'fore, so can't be from 'round here. Plenty of out of town-ers these days, so no surprise there."

"Oh?" I said.

"And not'a sign of the other guy you mentioned. He must be awn the inside somewhere."

"Did you get a name or anything?" I asked. "While at Frank's?"

He faced down disappointingly in thought. "Nope, no name."

"And you're sure that's the guy?"

"Oh, yes, sure am. Even from at 'distance, can't mistake his tapered top, rotund body."

I watched Flip become uncomfortable. It seemed he was putting two and two together. Somehow, he knew the other man might be Eliot.

From what Flip had told me, it made sense. The guy needed someone to help him, a local perhaps, to show him the water. Asking around the bait shops was as good a place as any. Always common knowledge that people who made livings on the water knew it better than most—especially mullet fishermen.

I stepped to the bow, swiped fish scales off my legs, and brushed them from my arms. Afternoon began to fade, and the sightless moon had a steady lift on the water level.

"What's the plan now?" Flip asked.

"I'm not sure at this moment."

Flip reversed the Sheffield and banked the mangroves.

"I tell you what," I said. "It looks like, for now anyway, that this head-goon needs Klinger, at least for a little while longer." I pointed toward the narrow creek where my skiff sat with a sliced fuel line. "Let's head over toward that creek. I want to check on my boat … since it's close."

"Sounds right b'me," Flip replied. "Ya'gawna lay down awn my mullet again?"

"Nah, I think we'll be able to sneak in without getting seen."

"Gotcha." Flip set the engine in gear, and we made for the creek.

"Are you good on fuel?" I asked.

"Oh, yeah, filled'er up this morning, can run *allll* day."

As we neared the creek, I kept my eyes fixed on the fish shack, careful to ensure we remained hidden and didn't suddenly appear in plain view. The last thing we needed was to be spotted motoring toward the very boat those thugs had just battered—it would only spark needless suspicion.

I eyed Flip. He stood bone dry wearing yellow fishing waders held up by suspenders, of which showed his experience as a mullet fisherman, and a Floridian. I was also confident that, from me, he didn't need navigational advice when routing through the creek. He should have no problem dodging multiple centered shoals or the sunken oyster beds edging below the mangrove roots. He knew these waters about as well as anyone could. For people who dared to make their living on the water, there was a certain confidence they needed to equip. Fear had something to do with it—or the lack of it. A certain attribute that seemed to come standard to any human who would rather be outdoors than stuck inside, that they would, in time, become attracted to the sea. People like Flip, and the ones who knew life beyond fear, see the opposite side, the ending. They see the sea for more than just monetary gain; they see it for its vast scholarly offerings and crave to preserve it. For Man, there was more to learn out on the water than most land-based encounters. One would have to look to the stars to find a greater database of wisdom.

Rounding the last switchback, I said, "My skiff should be coming into view after this last point."

Approaching the skiff, the strong scent of fuel caused me to cringe, and the expression on Flip's face was no surprise.

"Damn, that's strong," he noted.

"Yeah, about dumped fifteen gallons into the bilge."

"You weren't lyin', huh? How big your bilge? Prolly filled to the brim."

"I'm not so sure. Ten gallons seems about right."

Flip drifted the Sheffield port to port beside the skiff. After lifting a long pipe from under the gunwale, he pinned his boat in place using the homemade fiberglass anchor stick.

Back at the stern, I lowered into the chest-high water, waded to the skiff, and heaved aboard. At the center console, I found my wallet, but missing the little cash I had, and of course my I.D.

Flip began regarding the bilge. "Where'd it cut at?"

I reached for the prime bulb, found it, and presented Flip the severed hose. "Right here."

Flip's face said it all. "Unbelievable … now, why'd someone need to go awn and do somethin' like that?"

"To disable me, that's why, or at least slow me down."

"I should say so, shaa-ame."

I waved the sliced hose. "So, what do you think?"

He removed a shade hat and scratched his peach-fuzzed head. "Hmm … w'ale … let me think…"

"Hey, do me a favor? While you work magic on the hose, I need to go and check something out. I'll be right back."

"W'ale … um … sure." Flip leaned to his stern, opening compartments. "Might have somethin' we can use in one of these hatches."

"Cool, thanks. I'll just be a minute." I dismounted and inspected the water while I carefully waded fifty feet to the small bank.

The semi-sparse, bushy entry point we'd used earlier was still passable, so I climbed onto a fallen tree and pushed through the first tangle of thin mangroves. The tide had nearly swallowed our earlier path, but after a quick adjustment, it actually became easier to navigate.

I peeked for signs of those hogs, and for balance, instinctively anchored a foot on a dry log, when out of the corner of my eye, a peculiar object caught my attention. It was the same branch I had used earlier to secure the water moccasin.

Feeling dumbfounded, I reached for the branch, lifting it from the water. To my amazement the snake was still stuck—and alive! It squirmed and coiled, desperate to free its fangs from the mangrove husk.

I hurried back the way I came, taking with me the branch and snake. Finally, I popped through the last mangrove, keeping the snake well ahead of me while it wormed its way along the branch. I continued sloshing to the boats. Flip had his head down in the bilge.

"Any luck?" I asked.

"W'ale, I think I found something we could—" He froze and peeked up. "What'n the hell you got there?"

I held out the branch like a prize. "It's a snake on a stick, and it's our only weapon."

19

Eliot thought to himself while alone in the fish shack.

I was hoping the weather would be clearing up by now. It'll be dark in a couple hours. C'mon phone—ring. This whole thing has turned out to be one big ol' disaster. All I wanted was to make a few bucks to pay bills. Maybe Klinger is right, we should take Lester out. Not kill, oh no ... that one would be a hard one for God to forgive, and I'm not willin' to test it, but just enough to escape and call the police. Or even go 'round Cape Haze Point and find Flip. I know he'd still be fishin' in this weather. He's a good friend.

****

Klinger had been pumping strendously for nearly twenty minutes, emptying the small boat of rainwater. He stood.

Lester asked, "You about done, boy?"

Klinger said nothing, but attempted to de-board.

"Hold it right there!" Lester said, rising off the chair. "Did I say you were finished?"

Klinger sulked, re-boarded the Whaler while Lester wobbled down the three steps to the dock, which creaked under pressure.

The rain had subsided enough, leaving Lester clear from an inconvenient soaking. He crept forward to the uneven cuts of the planks, peering into the small boat. Klinger stood while dripping wet and held the pump.

"I suppose that's good enough," Lester said. "But it's your duty to make sure it stays that way, got it?"

"Wha'ever…"

Lester glanced in the direction he saw the fishing boat a short while ago. He then made his way up the dock steps to his chair and motioned Klinger inside.

Klinger breezed past and sat on the bunk across from Eliot. Soon after sitting, rainwater snaked along his leg onto the floor, pooling into a small puddle.

Eliot glanced up and cracked a halfhearted smile.

"Not funny, man," Klinger said gruffly. "I'm freezin'."

Eliot leaned in, whispering, "What's the weather lookin' like out there?"

Klinger shrugged crossly. "Wha'you *think* it looks like, man? I's nasty out there and fixin' t'get nastier!"

Lester passed through the shack's doorway and examined the small countertop next to the sink. Eliot and Klinger both watched warily while Lester emptied his pockets onto the counter. Out came Klinger's can of Copenhagen, his knife, and wallet. Eliot's wallet and the stolen license came next, which he snapped onto the counter. Next, he pulled out Eliot's cell phone, flipped it open, extended his arm, focused on the screen, read it, and folded it closed. He laid the gun on the table next to the knife.

After satisfied all contents of his packets had emptied onto the counter, Lester stuffed the gun first into the side pocket of his overalls, tucked it snugly, and loaded the other items into his side pockets. Eliot's wallet and cell phone he gave back.

"Here, take this. Make sure you pay attention to it now. You don't want to be missing any calls. Got it?"

Eliot accepted the things while in total surprise. *Why is he handing me the phone back? Now he's giving it back? Something isn't right.* He leaned on the bunk, opened the phone, closed it, peeked at Klinger, and slid it inside his camouflaged pocket.

Klinger became puzzled, mouthed, "What the hell, man?" He then shifted in his seat and said to Lester, "Can I have m'can of dip ... please?"

Lester reflected briefly, slung the can of Copenhagen at Klinger, who snagged it before hitting the wooden-studded wall.

"T'anks." Klinger proceeded to pack the can, popping his index finger over the silver lid. He didn't wait but a moment to pinch out a wad, centering it cozily in his lower front lip, all while he held the can underneath to catch the spilling strands. After closing the lid, he rammed the can down his soaked pocket, reached for his empty water bottle, and spat into it.

Eliot observed in disgust as the brown spittle trickled down the inside of the bottle.

Klinger settled back as the nicotine did its job to increase his heart rate, raise his blood pressure, and provide him with an overwhelming sense of satisfaction. "Man—oh—man," he mumbled. "Could I go for a spliff right 'bout now."

Eliot shook his head. *Disgustin'.*

Klinger leaned, bulging lip and all, toward Lester. The nicotine rush had injected him with courage. "What's all this stuff for anyway … box in mill' of nowhere? What's 'at 'bout?"

Lester closed his eyes and breathed deep but said nothing. He slipped through the threshold and faced out to the incoming storm, blocking the gray outside light, creating a dark silhouette.

Klinger's voice rose, projecting it toward the door. "So 'at box is for you, huh?"

Lester turned. "What did you say, boy?"

"I'm just wonderin' what's in the box, is all."

Lester clacked his teeth and stepped into the house, gripping the gun handle against his side as though it were a cane. "You listen up, and you listen close, you got no business knowing what any of this stuff is. You got it? You keep pokin' at my last nerve. If you think you can keep playin' this little game of yours, then you've got another thing comin.' Oh, yeah … these people picking up this package do *not* mess around. They will kill you and your whole dam family."

Klinger shrugged off the threat and left a smirk on his face.

Eliot's jaw tightened. *Shut up, kid. You'll get us both killed.*

Lester picked up Klinger's wallet from the counter. "So, where're you from, boy?"

Klinger said proudly, "Right 'ere, Charr-lotte County."

"Oh, you don't say…?"

"Ye-up."

Lester flipped opened the wallet. "You got any family here, Klinger … Nowell?" He read the license, shutting one eye, adjusting, focusing the distance for his bad eyes.

"Um … nope … jus' me."

"You're telling me that you're *from* here, but have no family *here*? And live in the…" Lester again squinted, reading the small letters on the license. "…Ranchettes?"

Klinger shifted in his seat. "'As right."

"Hmm…" He grinned. "I most definitely doubt that." Lester slung the wallet open and slipped out Klinger's picture book and tossed the wallet on the counter. His thumb-flipped through the clear plastic pages, said, "You're tellin' me that *these* children in *these* pictures are not related to *you*?"

Klinger eyes pulsed, and he tried to control the erupting anger. His grip was slipping away. He swallowed hard. "Nope."

"That's very interesting. If I would happen to show up at … let's see…" Lester held up the license again. "Orange Grove Avenue? I wouldn't find a wife and a couple of beautiful kids—"

Klinger no longer held himself back. He hadn't the ability and leaped forward and rushed toward the man.

Eliot expected Klinger's rage and had positioned himself between the two at the right moment. Before Klinger could paw a hand on Lester, Eliot wrangled him downward, pinning him in a standing full nelson.

In Klinger's justifiable violence, he kicked out his feet. "I'll kill your ass if yah ever come near m'family! You hear me, man?"

Lester jerked the gun out from his pocket, moved forward, and pointed it at Klinger's nose—not more than a foot away, this time he thumbed back the hammer.

A saucer-eyed Klinger breathed hard, snarling in torrents of rage.

Eliot maneuvered Klinger aside to avoid the spray of brain if Lester decided to pull the trigger. *Please … don't do it. Jesus help me*, he thought. *Right now, I drink from the chalice of your blood.*

Lester said with threatening patience, "You just don't get it, do you? These people will kill your whole family, boy. You'd better just act appropriate and do what I say, and this will be all over soon—"

Tobacco strands spewed from Klinger's mouth as he shouted, "You bet' not come near m'family, man. I'm warnin' you!" His kicks were vicious at Lester's hand holding the gun, but his foot hit only air.

"I want nothing to do with your family, boy! All I need is to get this pain-in-the-ass package where it needs to go, and that's it. You keep pressing buttons and I might snap, got it? Keep pulling my hair. I dare you!"

Klinger remained silent, clenched his jaw, delineating angry facial muscles.

Eliot held on, frustrated, waiting for a sign of surrender, or instructions from Lester.

Lester now seized Klinger's eyes and centered the gun. Frustration glazed in his eyes as he attempted to sap Klinger's will. "Don't fuck with *me*, boy!"

Klinger lowered his head and loosened up.

It was soundless for two minutes, except for the light rain on the roof.

Lester, after a brief cool down, motioned using the gun to release Klinger.

Eliot, in his camouflage pants, looking like a soldier rather than a mullet fisherman, untangled his arms and freed Klinger.

Klinger jerked his shoulders and twisted as though he had freed himself. He sat his saturated body onto the bunk, breathing hard, snatched the dip bottle, and spat. Dried, crisp tobacco juice cornered his mouth.

"Both of you!" Lester added.

Eliot's six-foot-four-inch frame sat five feet across on the bunk bed and folded his arms. After a few moments had passed, he studied Lester's mannerisms— the increased breathing, the slight tremble in his hand, and concluded Klinger had significantly raised the man's blood pressure.

Lester moved to the doorway and pulled out smokes, lit one, and exhaled. Before stepping through the doorway, he pulled one more drag before arching a peek in at the men.

The rain now entered a lighter phase, to a soothing, soft tap on the tin roof.

Eliot's expression dimmed as he faced Klinger. *Can't he just not say anything else?*

Klinger made sure the short, chubby man was gone before speaking to Eliot. "Thanks for 'at help back 'air … I could've taken 'em out, man!"

"What you just did was almost get yourself killed!"

Klinger licked the dried tobacco from the corner of his mouth. "I had 'em right where I needed 'em, man."

"I surely doubt that, no sir."

"I could've taken 'at fat ass out. I've rolled hogs bigger'n him, easy!"

"Sure … uh-huh," Eliot said. "He got the gun, remember?"

"W'got do somepin quick, man. He ain't lettin' me or *you* jus' walk awn out 'ere."

"You got to calm yourself."

Klinger sat fidgeting, whispered, "Hey, man? How much yah gettin' paid for this anyhow?"

"Doesn't matter," Eliot replied.

"Sure it do … i's a motive t'kill yah. I know he'll kill me, 'cause I'm a loose end."

Consideration set in as Eliot leaned backward. *Lester gave me my phone back … so that's got to mean somethin'.*

Klinger asked, "Five hund'ed? A thousand?"

"Five," Eliot answered.

Klinger's expression changed to confusion. "Five hund'ed … 'at's it?"

"Thousand," Eliot corrected.

Klinger's cheeks dropped, and his tone changed. "Hmmm, dang … 'at's lot of bread."

"Yeah, and I need the money really bad. Like I say before … real bad."

"See, 'at just don't make no sense … to keep yah 'round, I mean."

"You sayin' he's killin' me, and then stealin' my half?"

"At's exactly what I'm sayin' to you, man."

Wood creaks and footsteps pattered as Lester waddled further out onto the deck surrounding the shack.

With Lester out of earshot, Eliot leaned toward Klinger, removed his shades, revealing a sharp nose and bulging, dove-like eyes. "Don't you got a family? Why you keep actin' this way? If you just shut your mouth and do what he says, you'll get yourself out of here no problem … hmm?"

"Yeah, I got fam'ly." Klinger's shoulders lowered, went at ease, said woefully, "… five great kids—age ten, eight, seven, four, and six'month."

Eliot's voice lowered. "See, that's what you got to do this for—calm yourself."

Klinger didn't mull for long. "You? Fam'ly?"

"Sure do. Got a son and a daughter—both awn to college soon … first ones in our family."

"Wife?"

"Oh, yeah. Janet—she's the love of my life. Got sick a few years ago, though, and it's been tough … money-wise—needs help gettin' 'round, and without her income, and the way the mullet business is goin', I need this extra money … get it? You can understand that?"

"How'd yah come to find this gig anyway? Don't seem like it would be posted awn the work wall at Frank's or anythin'."

"There's a certain brotherhood that mullet guys have. We look out for one another. Lester started askin' around at local bait shops if anyone was lookin' for extra work. My good buddy Flip told me about it so—"

"Flip Peas?"

The connection surprised Eliot. "Um … well, yes, Flip Peas. How'd you—"

"'At's where I know yah!" Klinger snapped his fingers. "I always knew yah was familiar, just couldn't place yah. He's m'good buddy's neighbor. Saw 'em this mornin' loadin' up his boat … gettin' ready to head out."

Eliot did a Lester check, glancing toward the door, then leaned back to Klinger. "I saw him along the Cape Haze Point coast while we were still on the *Itinerant.*"

Klinger nodded and eased a satisfying smile. "We seen you guys … floatin' off Cape 'aze Point, too."

"Well…" Eliot had a moment of thought, became disparaged, shook his head. "When yous were at the crate, I was shocked to see Shamus. Oh, man, he's gonna think down about me…"

"Nah, he won't. You just doin' what yah had to do."

For a moment, both men sat silent, understanding their allied connection.

Eliot said, "Yes, we were waiting for the plane to call. I had no idea this was the job. If I had known, I'd of said no way."

Klinger shook his head in agreement.

"I just figured he was new in town and needed a guide for the day ... just to learn the waters an all. Maybe throw some net. I knew I'd catch some static from the other mullet guys ... you know, helping out a traveler. But I needed the money."

"So, you guy's jus' met today?"

"Yeah, this morning ... at the boat ramp."

"Ponce de Leon Park?"

Eliot shook his head. "You guys should've stayed far, far away."

"Yeah, beginin' to think 'at might'a been a *good* idea."

Eliot took a deep breath. "You listen up," he began. "A mullet fisherman's job's not for the soft-skinned, okay? Rain or shine, bills must be paid, yup, so money's gotta keep flowin'. Mullet prices are about eighty cents a pound, commercially, and only the plump, roe-filled females garner above a dollar'a pound. Bringin' in a couple hundred pounds average a day is necessary for me to live. That's if I'can even sell my catch entirely. Foreign countries importin' cheap knock-offs usin' farm-raised fish pose stiff competition and hurt us local fishermen, yup. Never mind the stigma that mullet have.

People get off-put by a minor oily factor and compared it to catfish, or other throwaway fishes."

Klinger was at full attention.

"Having a family puts an even greater financial strain on me, yup. I'd been in this business m'whole life, and now I'm pushin' fifty-six, thinkin' 'bout a retirin' plan. M'kids are enterin' college on minimal financial aid, wife is sick, and I've got m'own discouragin' medical issues, too: bad knees, bad back, arthritis-riddled fingers, and painful neck kinks, yup. The extra five thousand dollars could go a long way for me and my family."

Klinger nodded sadly.

*****

Outside, Lester walked the backside perimeter of the fish shack, calming himself after the health-detrimental episode with Klinger. He sucked a drag from his smoke, focused out to a driveway-sized island a few hundred yards south, and removed the Zippo. Clinking it open and closed a few times, he clenched his jaw, felt the jaw muscle knot, coughed, and flicked the cigarette into the water. He seemed calm enough, and sending creaks throughout the deck, paced back to the frontside of the shack.

Klinger clenched at the returning footsteps and glanced at Eliot, then to the door. The footsteps ended inches before entering the doorsill. Eliot turned his head and held his breath.

"I still think we need to break awn free, man," Klinger whispered in a hurry. "You a bi-i-i-g guy. Should 'ave no trouble knockin' 'em out."

Eliot got the last word. "Will you just relax and follow along? That's our best chance, yup."

Lester entered the small Turtle Bay fish shack, skimming over both men. A conversation showed on their faces, but Lester shrugged it off, sat back in the doorway chair—half in, half out.

Klinger eyes circled, looking up, down. He wanted a plan—saw the TV/VCR combo. He looked toward the sink, at the wooden walls, over at Lester sitting in the chair blocking their escape. He focused in on the tin roof, eyeing the tiny metal circles of nail heads.

"I gotta take a wiz," he said.

Lester shifted in his seat to the condescending lip. "What did you say?"

Klinger repeated, "Said ... I *gotta* take a *wiz*."

"A wizz?"

"Yeah. *A wiz*."

Lester closed his eyes.

Eliot had patience, waited for a response, certain Klinger's head was about to get blown off.

Lester closed his eyes, as though saying a prayer. He opened and reached for his gun. "Go right ahead."

Klinger stood, approached the doorway using small, careful steps.

Eliot watched Lester reach for the gun. *This is it ... don't do it, kid,* he thought as Klinger glided up behind Lester.

To face Klinger, Lester swiveled his neck. It was like a telepathic standoff when their eyes met. Lester suddenly gripped the gun, slipped it halfway from his pocket, eyes locked on Klinger's—a subliminal dare.

Klinger paused two feet from the man, eyeing the doorway.

Lester removed the gun from his pocket and eased his thumb to the hammer.

"W'ale?" Klinger said.

Lester replied with an edge, "Well … what?"

"W'ale—can yah move?"

Lester's edge yielded. His weight shifted in the chair.

Klinger scraped past him onto the deck below the roof's eave, long-stepped along the perimeter deck—one that he thought was sneaky.

"Ahh, hold it right there. That's far enough."

Klinger ignored and managed another foot. If he moved further out, the eave of the roof would no longer protect him from the inexorable rain. His eyeballs spun.

Lester from behind, stared back at him, tapping the gun on the cheap metal armrest.

"Uh—hello?" Klinger said.

"Something wrong, boy?"

"Can I get a lil' priv'cy?"

"If you gotta go, you better go. You got *two* minutes."

Klinger faced forward, unzipped, and began mumbling, "Man, I need'a get outta 'ere." He focused straight ahead, following the perimeter deck to the corner. "Real easy, jus' jump and swim. B'like livin' off the land."

Klinger finished and zipped up. Before turning, he inspected along the perimeter deck.

Lester greeted him with an arrogant, cocky smile. "Well … all done?"

"Ye-up."

"Good."

Klinger brushed past Lester while entering the shack and sat back onto the bunk.

This time Lester stood, followed him in, to the sink, opening the cabinet below the countertop. He bent over pawing at something.

Klinger and Eliot shrugged at each other.

Lester emerged holding out a wad of zip-ties. He removed two single tie wraps and zeroed in on the tiny ends, noting which ends were what, the male or female. He finally figured it out and connected two—concocting a larger one.

Klinger tensed.

"Come here, boy."

Klinger stood.

Lester glared at him; jaw clenched. "Get over here. Now."

Klinger leaned forward, paused.

"Slow!" Lester snapped. "Nice and slow … and hold out your wrists."

Again, Klinger resisted a step forward. "Wha'is for?"

"Do you think I'm stupid, boy? I saw you out there. You were thinking about running for it, weren't you?"

"No—"

"Don't lie to me. Hold out your wrists!"

Klinger extended his arms defiantly, swung his wrists before Lester's chest. He eyed Lester's short, stubby fingers, fumbling the restraints. Lester's index fingers, stained yellow from smoking, picked at the male-end of the tie, finding it, and zipping it tight. When finished, he gripped the gun.

"Now sit!"

Klinger held still. "For what?"

Eliot's hand snuck along the outside of his thigh pocket and caressed the knife he had stolen from the tackle box aboard the rank *Itinerant*. He thought about setting Klinger free, cutting the makeshift handcuffs but decided it wouldn't be smart. Upsetting Lester might damage his side of the cash—especially so close to the finish. Eliot's eyes lifted, and he half-grinned toward Klinger.

Lester snuck a few steps near the doorjamb and sat.

Now tied up, Klinger shook his head in embarrassment while Eliot sat with folded arms.

20

After wading back to my skiff, I exposed the snake to Flip. He saw it stuck to the stick from a safe distance. He twisted from a kneeled position over the bilge to inspect the snake's head.

"Where'd ya'find that thing?"

"Earlier today, when Klinger and I were investigating the falling object, this little guy tried to bite me, so I pinned him to a dead branch. Stayed exactly where I'd left him, still attached so…"

"This day keeps awn gettin' stranger and stranger." Flip scowled while the snake squirmed and coiled. "Well, you jus' keep that unforgivin' demon snake the hell'way from me, okay?"

"No problem." I wedged the branch under my boat's gunwale into an empty rod holder and pinned the push pole beside it. Once satisfied, I waded to the stern to check on Flip's progress. "Any luck?"

"W'ale, I was able t'splice the two ends together, but can't make'er airtight."

He had used a piece of PVC pipe and coupled the two severed hose ends and zip-tied them tight—not a bad fix.

Flip's head lifted from the small bilge, aware of his surrounding, to avoid the poling platform. He seeemd wary of the snake, making sure it wasn't near him, asked, "How much fuel yah say was in your fuel cell?"

"About fifteen gallons," I answered.

Flip lifted onto his knees, to his feet, sheening his yellow wading suspenders in fuel. Profuse sweat dripped off his face. "Might be lot easier if I jus' towed yah."

"Under different circumstances, I'd say let us get the hell out of here. Towing me is just not an option."

"Even if this jerry-rig works, and your engine will run, yah might not be able to even get'er awn plane…" He scratched his head. "With the bilge full of fuel and all."

"Yeah, I was thinking the same thing."

"There's so much fuel, Shamus. Seems the only smart thin' would be comin' back with a few five-gallon tanks and pumpin'er dry."

"Smart is right…" I mumbled, then pointed to my bilge. "Is all that fuel? Any saltwater?"

"Ta'me looks like all fuel, smells like it too, but wit'all this rain, I'd say some rain, but most of it fuel."

I raised my chin toward his aluminum fuel cell. "How much fuel would you say you burned today? Any chance you have room in your cell for a few gallons?"

"Hmm," he answered, scratching his head. "I suppose, le'me check and see."

Flip waded to his boat and reached under the console for the gas stick. He unscrewed the metal cap and inserted the stick until it hit bottom. Focusing in on the marks, he said, "Look like I'm 'bout five gallons down."

"So, you can fit five more gallons?"

"I would say so, sure."

"Okay," I said, rising in confidence. "All we need now is some spare bilge hose."

As if I didn't need to suggest it, Flip managed out ten feet of spare hose from his front hatch. Common for guys making their living on the water to carry spares of everything. He handed it to me.

"Now, I know what yah thinkin', and I'm not so sure w'can transfer that amount into my tank without spillin' some," he explained. "And runnin' that amount of fuel through your bilge pump … gawna ruin it, and may blow us all to hell."

To myself, I weighed the risks. "I'm willing to replace the bilge pump later, you know that. If this salty fuel damages anything to your engine, I'll gladly reimburse you."

Flip just shook his head with a somber understanding. We both paused, mulling different ideas in our heads. The idea of pumping tainted fuel into his fuel cell wore thin. I decided not to damage his boat if I could help it.

"Okay, I have a better idea," I said. "Do you have a cup … or a small bucket? A pail maybe? Something I can bail out the water from my baitwell?

"Oh, yeah, sure do—here, try'is." He handed me a silver scoop used for chum.

"That will work perfect."

I lifted into my skiff, opened the fourteen-gallon surface-mounted front baitwell, and began bailing the water. My plan was to pump the tainted fuel into the baitwell, to level out the center of gravity and allow the skiff to ease on plane.

"Those were some nice ones, huh?" Flip noted as I saddened while dumping the greenbacks overboard.

He lifted his chin. "Cape 'aze Point?"

"Yes, sir ..." I watched the bait swim away. "They sure were some good ones."

I finished bailing the water and slipped the spare hose into the baitwell. Now at the bilge, I knelt, leaned over the stern, took the other end of the hose, and slid it deep into the bilge exhaust. It needed to be a tight fit. Not sure the hose had been secured, I slid back into the waist-deep water.

My angle on the bilge exhaust improved, and I wrapped the slack once around the poling platform to secure the hose. Still in the water, I extended an arm, stretching to reach the bilge pump switch on the console switch panel.

Flip snuck a few steps back. "Easy now."

The explosion factor was real, and I squinted pressing the switch, sending three amps to the small pump.

At first, nothing except the whine of a small spinning propeller. It began to bog after a few seconds.

Flip gave a thumbs up, and aware of the danger, cautiously peeked at the tank. "She's a flowin' all right."

"You see it?"

"Yup, can see it flowin' awn in."

"Seems good back here, too," I added, noting small drops that had rainbowed onto the water's surface.

In minutes, a fuel/watery mix filled the entirety of the clear baitwell. I'd made a ballsy move to pump the fuel through a bilge pump, which wasn't rated for fuel. When the baitwell became filled to the brim, I switched off the bilge pump and heaved into the skiff. Now with a full baitwell and an empty bilge, from earlier trips, I knew the boat would reach an easy plane with the perfect balance. I removed the spare hose and handed it back to Flip.

"What now?" he asked, climbing into his boat.

"First, I'd like to see the engine stays running. The whole plan counts on it. I figure with the amount of fuel burned this morning, and the amount that spilled, based on a seventeen-gallon tank, I estimate there is … about one … two gallons remaining in mt cell. Just enough to end this and get the hell home."

"Agreed," he said, squinting as I reached for the key.

At my console, and due to Flip's seniority among us, I gave him a last second glance. He grinned from his helm, nodded the go-ahead, and with a tightly clenched anal sphincter, I turned the key. The engine cranked but didn't start.

"Check awn the primer bulb," Flip shouted from behind his console. "You need t'keep that hard so ya'gawna have to keep checkin' awn it. Like I said, air's gettin' in, so to keep the pressure up, squeeze awn it a minute."

I reached back and pumped the black bulb until hardened with fuel, not super hard like normal, but fuel was flowing. I cranked the engine again—it started, then sputtered silent.

"Keep tryin' it," he said.

I cranked it longer and the engine popped to life, settling back to a strong idle. "Okay, let's go."

"Where to?" Flip asked.

"Um…" His question made me hesitate, my apprehension piqued. I wasn't sure if my choices were right—but we had to keep moving. Now, with Flip looking to me for answers—unlike our usual dynamic— I drew a deep breath and took the lead. "Let's motor out of this creek and into the open water. Remember where we stopped earlier, about three hundred yards on the other side of the bay?"

"Out'ta site of the fish shack, right?"

"Yup, right there. Let's meet there again."

Flip nodded.

I eased the engine in gear, though any faster would cause a stall.

We progressed out from the creek at a tick past idle, which rolled up a decent size wake, bowling it to shore, lifting mangroves overhangs. Red submerged roots allowed the green leaves to come to rest onto the water's surface.

As we rounded the switchbacks, passing the now sunken logs, the oyster beds were no longer visible. The tide had now met the high-water mark.

We exited the narrow creek in tandem. I eased up the throttle. The skiff sped and settled on plane.

Engine sputtering began again, and my instincts inched it passed half-throttle. I checked on Flip behind. He was waving his arm, squeezing his hand into a fist.

I reached blindly behind me, grasping for the primer ball. When it filled, fuel pressure increased—stabilizing the engine's hum. I gave Flip the thumbs up.

As we moved on, I admired the enormous storm encompassing Turtle Bay and wondered if the sky would ever be clear again. Would I ever see blue again? The pouring rain ahead reduced our visibility down to a few hundred feet. I checked on the snake. The gentle rocking of the boat seemed to startle it into a tense, unmoving stillness.

We arrived at the spot, and I lowered the boat off plane. Flip swept up behind me.

We sat afloat for seconds while the fish shack sat just out of view. I decided to maneuver the boat closer to the mangroves to gain a bit more coverage. Now positive I couldn't be seen from the shack, I waved Flip over, and we lashed together.

I asked, "Hey, you mind sticking your anchor stick down?"

"Will do," Flip replied, then stretched back, anchoring his boat, keeping our vessels stationary.

"What we gawna do now?" he asked.

"Well, I know one thing's for sure—I need to sneak to the rear of the fish shack without getting seen."

"Rear? What you need awn the backside?"

"I know a perimeter deck surrounds it, and from what you said, I doubt they're watching it. It's a good spot to surprise them."

Flip straightened the wheel and adjusted the lash lines. "You gonna walk awn up and jus' ask for yah buddy back?"

"I haven't thought it out that far."

"W'ale, if we ride the back way, that might take a few extra minutes. With the tide, might be 'en easy ride."

Flip's suggestion would take us all the way into Bull Bay, to make a time-costing loop.

"Um…" I said. "I don't think I have enough fuel for that. It'll take us all the way into Bull Bay. Klinger doesn't have that kind of time, and I don't want to risk it."

"Okay … I see."

I saw a ponder cross Flip's eyes.

Eliot, I thought, and then pointed. "I think that southern mangrove point over there will provide us some good cover."

Flip gazed out to the windy bay.

I said, "Hand me those binoculars?"

"Right here." Flip reached into the rear hatch, passed them over to me.

At the bow, I lowered to a seated position and plunged into waist-high water.

Flip's eyes questioned me.

I said, "I'm going to take a quick wade to the point over there." I thumbed over to the tip of a mangrove outcrop. "See if I can get a better look at the shack. The last thing I want is for him to see us crossing back down to the south."

The mangrove outcrop was fifty feet along the tree line. Sharp shards of oysters crackled under my feet. After adjusting my footing, I raised the binoculars to my eyes. Like looking through two keyholes, I peered through the binoculars and squinted to see through the falling rain. Klinger stood on the far end of the perimeter deck pissing off the deck into the bay. The gunman sat on the threshold, keeping a jailer's watch. Klinger stepped toward the chaired man and into the cabin.

"Hmmm," I muttered. "Klinger must be finished bailing water from the small boat." I decided the window had opened.

I plowed back through the waist-deep water using such force that it sank my calves into the muck. The oysters provided adequate traction at times though, but I cringed at the thought of slicing open a boot, exposing pale flesh to the seawater, so I slowed a bit. Maintaining a firm, but steady pace was the best method for wading through this type of varying terrain under my feet. I reached the boat, hopped up, and swung in.

"Looks like we've got a window ... a small one."

Flip asked, "They still takin' cover in the fish shack?"

"Yup, still are. Klinger stood on the dock while the gunman kept a watch. If I had to guess, I'd say the other guy's still on the inside while this next thunderhead passes." I pointed at the dark cloud above. "So we've got to move."

Flip removed the fiberglass pipe from the mud and stowed it under his gunwale, next to a reeking pile of dead mullet. "What's plan from here awn?"

"Simple, really. Now that they're inside, we can make a run for it."

"Run for it?"

"It's now or never. I have a feeling the next break in the rain, they're leaving the fish shack ... and their probable destination is the *Itinerant*. At that point, it might be too late to get Klinger back."

"I see," Flip said, finger-combing his beard. "Sound kinda bold, don't yah think?"

Flip's unconfident agreement brought the seriousness out of what I was about to attempt.

I stayed focused. "What we need to do is haul *ass* ... stick to the east side of Turtle Bay ... try not to draw attention to ourselves. We must do it incognito, or the whole plan goes to hell. The next rendezvous point will be back behind the house on the southern side. I know of a small island we can stop behind, to provide cover one last time, before I attempt a rescue."

"Know 'at island well," Flip said, nodding nervously.

"Yup. It's about five hundred yards from the south side of the fish shack." I eased back behind the wheel of my skiff. "I hope my engine stays running until we get there."

Flip reached for his boat's key ring, which was a de-hooked red lure and cranked his engine to life. "I don' see why it shouldn't. It's only a'mile."

"We shall see." I turned the ignition, and the engine sputtered but settled to idle. "I'll lead."

As I approached the thinning-end of the mangroves, exposing us to the fish shack, I reached back again and gave the primer bulb a preemptive pump.

Giving Flip one last check, I applied pressure on the throttle and the engine RPMs reached a firm four thousand. The skiff glided along. Behind, Flip had also reached plane.

I clamped the stainless-steel wheel and palmed the steering knob. On the tree limb, the moccasin seemed snug. It had wound around the branch and had wedged into a corner.

A thick wall of unavoidable rain a quarter mile ahead looked like two closing curtains. I tapped the binnacle arm, reaching wide-open throttle. The RPMs spiked upwards of six thousand. Soon before we entered the wall of rain, I once again checked Flip, who followed behind at a safe distance. I glanced at the fish shack, a half-mile away, on starboard—its perimeter deck remained empty, but the shack door was open wide with no one in sight.

Cold raindrops smacked the front of the *Buff*, soaking it through, filtering me a drink of sweat and freshwater mix. Behind, Flip was hunching under his T-top, drier than a Death Valley summer, and looked similar to gazing out a rain-pelted window.

The downpour made the snake stir and squiggle—but it remained pinned. I realized with no landmarks or the still water surrounding sandbars to use as depth markers, my run through the shallow, sketchy bay would be blind.

As soon as I began to appreciate the danger of piloting a vessel sightless, the rain lightened, visibility improved, and to the south, holes of blue sky appeared through the thinning clouds.

My sight slowly cleared but I had accidentally veered off track—closer to the fish shack. I changed course and aimed to the east, away from the storm. When I banked, the evenness of the engine drone suddenly became irregular. Panic inched its way into my mind, but I remembered the primer bulb. Over and over, I squeezed that ball, pleading for the engine to stay running. "NO, not now, not now!" I squeezed and squeezed, but the RPMs continued to plummet, lifting the bow, dropping me off plane. "No … no!" I pounded the control, nearly snapping the throttle rod, and again squeezed the bulb. But luck struck again, and it began to harden, fuel pressure climbed, which elevated the skiff back to a full-speed plane. "C'mon, baby!"

Only after the engine remained smooth and steady did I let out a breath. I squinted toward the fish shack—still clear.

For a moment, my attention wandered, and the skiff slapped an unseen broadside wave, sheathing the bow in frothy seawater, which slipped off the deck, overtop the snake, ending across my feet, splashing into the bilge, sloshing like bathwater.

I pounded through a short patch of chop. Halfway through the water-whoops, another rogue wave slammed the skiff. I failed to realize the snake branch had now joggled loose from the gunwale rod holder. I stomped on it, pinning it tight when it reached my foot.

I gripped the steering wheel eagle-tight, focusing a few yards ahead of the channel. "Almost through," I whispered intently.

Flip rode behind, persistent, a hundred feet off the stern, keen to my obstacles. I set sights on a small mangrove island on the southern wall of Turtle Bay. As it came into view, I realized I needed a clear, formulated plan to unite with Klinger and bring him back safe. Obviously, I couldn't walk up and knock on the door and expect to take my friend back.

After a short ride across the grass flats, centered in Turtle Bay, I reached the intended mangrove island and circled to the backside. Out of sight from the fish shack, I throttled back and spun the boat to face Flip, who was coming in hot. He lowered the boat, pushing a small wake. I circled it, and we met bow to bow.

"I didn't see anybody outside," I said and reached for the snake branch. "Me either," he said. "They look like they're awn the inside ... gettin' protection from the weather."

I clipped the snake branch into the gunwale rod holder. "I agree ... and I saw the small Whaler floating out front, so they're still in the house for sure."

Flip handled his anchor and pinned his boat stationary. I tossed him the bow rope, and he tugged my skiff close.

Blue sky was fighting to be seen. Gray clouds compressed again, and a brief rain shower hammered down as though it were the storm's grand finale. The skiff began to fill. I hated the idea of turning on the bilge pump and pumping the residual water/fuel mix into the bay, so I didn't.

My chance to save Klinger had arrived. I would use the unrelenting rain to my advantage. I knew sound didn't travel particularly well through rain. So I assumed mother nature would conceal my skiff's high-pitched engine drone.

Flip said above the rain, "W'ale, what's the plan? The last of the rain 'bout overhead now."

I curled a brow in his direction. "I know there's a hatch underneath the foundation…"

"Sure is." He cracked a smile. "—all'ese houses have 'em."

"Yup, so it's now or never." I gazed out toward the mangrove hedge that I wished to use as cover. "I'll motor halfway to that mangrove point, pole it from there, then sneak behind to the backside. Should be the last two hundred yards or so."

Flip took his wheel, seemed antsy. "Okay … sure sounds good 'nough."

From the look on Flip's face, I wouldn't ask him to follow. I'd run this part solo.

Flip asked, "Hey, Shamus, b'fore yah start a move awn, what did you say that other fella looked like? The one yah saw with the fat guy, near that fallin' box?"

"The tall guy?"

"Six-foot-four. Shaved head—looked to be about fifty-ish." I turned and faced the fish shack. "He was wearing camouflage pants." I couldn't play dumb anymore. I had to let him know who I meant. "It looked like Eliot."

Flip knew too, grinded his teeth and cussed under his breath. "You sure?"

Not having to keep that secret anymore steamed off the stress like a Florida asphalt after a summer downpour.

Flip looked at me oddly. His face frowned to a thinking man's. After a few seconds, he said, "Eliot's a big guy, prolly handle himself fine…"

"He is. And I'm pretty sure he won't argue with getting the hell out of there, either."

"You bet."

I turned away and said, "I'm heading to it. Seems like the rain might be letting up pretty soon, so…."

Flip seemed to be deep in thought, analyzing the info—cold stare, tight grip on the steering wheel. He broke free from his daze and snatched the blue bow line, untied it from his cleat and slung it atop the front deck.

I cranked the engine and stepped to the console. "Okay, Flip, I appreciate your help … really I do. Six pack, my treat, if, I mean *when* I make it back."

"I think I'll go awn and jus' hang back here … jus' incase."

"Are you sure? It might be dangerous—"

"Yeah … it's no pro'lem."

I smiled. "I do appreciate it. I promise to make it up to you."

Flip waved in confidence.

I geared the engine, idled off, and then rounded the mangrove island. A thousand yards away, the fish shack slipped into view. I headed straight for the mangrove tree line and figured I could hug along the bushes.

As I approached the tree line, a small break in the cloud beamed the sun onto the bay like a pinhole poked into the storm's bladder, spraying down a column of light. The way was now lit as the clouds thinned, yielding to the blue sky, letting radiant light penetrate the grayish white fluff. Parallel to the shore, below the water's surface, the sunlight opened a translucent world, exposing scattering mullet, grass beds, and out scurried a big snook, darting for auxiliary cover.

The ability for the rain to fall, and the sun to shine together was a Florida wonder. I closed in on the last outcrop of comforting refuge, dropped the skiff off plane, and deadened the engine. I sniffed the air. Down in the bilge, I noticed that additional fuel had leaked.

I released the seventeen-foot push pole from the deck clips and climbed onto the poling platform and pushed. The skiff glided off toward the mangrove outcrop. Here on out, I needed to remain silent.

At the point of full exposure, I faced back. Flip's image blurred, wearing the yellow waders, peeking from behind the island, watching me. I felt more comfortable of his solid favor by staying behind.

Moves were about to be made, intrepid, gunslinger moves, and in a good five seconds, I rethought the entire events that had led me here. To remain oriented, and to keep my morals positive was imperative. I had to remain calm, not frantic—fight it off—stay in control, block the panic. I had no time for my emotions to run amok. I deliberately shuddered my whole body, which helped to clear my guilt-ridden mind.

The skiff shifted forward when I drove the push pole deep into the sand and skirted the mangrove outcrop, out into the open. "Here we f-ing go…"

I used the skiff's momentum, adhering to a strict, uninterrupted pace. If anyone stepped out of the fish shack, since the stilts raised it much higher than sea level, I'd remain unseen. The current tidal elevation allowed a four-to-five-foot difference between the surface of the water and the shack's raised wooden foundation. I would only be visible if someone either walked along the rear perimeter deck or used the steps down to the small boat.

My heart pumped faster the closer I got to the Turtle Bay fish shack. The rain concealed my approach.

I made it to within feet of my cover spot below the shack when a man's voice echoed from the opposite side. I had nowhere to go, being out in the open, I was a sitting duck. All the gunman had to do was slip around the corner, and there I would be, plain as day. Even a novice shooter could pick me off.

In a near frantic, I hopped down from the poling platform. At the bow, push pole still in hand, I thrusted with all my might, sending the skiff pinpointing where I needed it, near the structure's far corner.

After the close call, I'd made it to a barnacle-encrusted corner piling. There, I knelt, waited, and listened, then felt shifting weight, heavy footsteps, and various minor reverberations. Bumping the shack now would no doubt blow my haphazardly planned rescue attempt to smithereens.

But so far, the plan had promise, and I began to loosen up and prepared next to progress and sneak underneath the house, where I'd arrive below the foundation. From there I could search for the hatch Klinger alluded to earlier in the day. To float the skiff underneath the shack had a high probability of ending badly, as the poling platform might only clear the floor joists by mere inches—but I went regardless.

I used my arms like crossing monkey bars to slide the entire skiff successfully under the house. The break in the rain felt wonderful, which brought my depleted senses a much-needed respite.

The wood was damp underneath and smelled like dirt from a hole. Like dirty balls of cotton, neat little spider webs tucked in the wooden corners. Roots from weeds laced tight to the crossbeams; some lucky enough to stretch to the edges where the light had bloomed them green. Rusted hooks bit deep into the wood, dangling fishing line tails from the pylons tops where the foundation began.

I found the hatch.

From above came movement, accompanied by voices. My hands were flat on the plywood floor. I felt around. The voices became louder. Someone stood at the front door under the roof's eave, and if they walked out further along the perimeter deck and down to the dock, they would no doubt see me. I braced—had nowhere to go. Those voices began talking, and then shuffling feet shocked me still. I was too late. They were coming out of the fish shack. I sensed it and slid behind the center piling to avoid gunfire.

One leg stepped down, then two, a camouflage pant leg—Eliot. Then a different set of pant legs, skinny—Klinger! They both carried the crate down the shack steps to the dock. White zip-ties bound Klinger's hands while he carried one end of the crate, and Eliot had the other. They each took baby steps, concentrating on footing as they shuffled along the slippery deck. Eliot first loaded into the Whaler, pulling the crate into position onto the bow. Klinger remained on the dock, adjusting the plastic handcuffs.

My whole body tightened as I awaited the gunman. The chances of him stepping to the lower docks without seeing me were good, but soon as any one of them turned and faced my direction, I'd be busted.

Klinger stood on the dock, his back toward my skiff. Eliot remained in the boat and adjusted, positioning the crate—then covered it using a blue tarp. He finished and stepped onto the dock.

They were coming back! There was no way they would miss me.

Klinger turned and froze. He spotted me beneath the shack, his mouth falling open in stunned silence. I raised a hand, palm out, then pointed upward. Pressing a finger to my lips, I whispered with a glance, 'Hatch.'"

He appeared to have recognized the sign. In his eyes, his shocked, frantic expression faded, a sign his cool would keep.

I sensed further movement from above—deep, heavy steps as the gunman stirred.

Klinger spun and relayed my instructions to Eliot— first, the stop-motion—second, the quiet signal. Eliot faced me after receiving the message. His expression didn't change, but his chin rose toward the doorway at attention, to the last person left.

21

Klinger followed Eliot in through the doorway after loading the crate. Both men slipped past Lester, who lingered on the deck. Klinger slid energetically onto the bunk, but well-mannered and disciplined. He spoke first as Eliot sat.

"Did ya'see 'em?" He glanced at the door. "Shamus?"

"Yeah, I seen him," Eliot whispered.

Klinger eyes pinned open as his endorphin levels spiked. "Look like he's come get me outta 'ere!"

Eliot said nothing, just flexed jaw muscles and tightened his lips. *He's really gonna ruinin' it for me. Now, I'm never gettin' paid. There is no way in hell Lester ain't seein' him down there. He'll shoot him dead, right there on his skiff. I pray Jesus has an answer for me—and him.*

Klinger slung up his zip-tied hands in a thrilled and eager manner. "I gotta get 'ese cut somehow, man."

Eliot shifted his hand to the side pocket on his pants, felt for the knife, but said nothing. *Why should I cut him free? He just ruined my payday. Put me in a very difficult position and all. Lester'll expect me to help him fight off Shamus. Not good, not good at all. Jesus, give me the strength...*

Klinger searched obsessively for something applicable to cut through the plastic handcuffs. His wrists were red and bled from moving the crate. "Gotta be somepin."

Heavy-footed steps creaked outside on the deck—a good signal Lester had slipped along the perimeter deck toward the rear of the fish shack.

Klinger said, "There got be somepin I can use in cuttin' 'ese,"—then remembered the knife on the table and began to stand.

Eliot grunted, "Don't! He'll notice that's missing the second he steps in the door, yup."

Klinger turned carefully. "Well, anything over 'air, on your side?"

"Oh hell," Eliot said and slung his knife toward Klinger's bunk.

Klinger's face went from surprised, to serious, to acceptance, and he snatched the knife, made a desperate attempt to slice his wrists free but struggled to start a cut.

Eliot checked the doorway, leaned in closer to Klinger, and said, "Just keep them lookin' like they still tied, okay?"

Klinger agreed, and due to his excitement, mishandled the knife and it slipped from his hands, landing a foot from his left leg. He extended it forward and pressed downward, dragging the knife toward him when his foot caught something underneath the thin, shabby carpet. He felt across the bump in the rug until he realized it was the lock to the hatch.

Klinger continued but struggled sawing through the plastic handcuffs. He kept pausing to listen, to get a bead on Lester's whereabouts.

Eliot watched in silence. *Only Jesus can save this man.* "Here, gimmie that." He reached for the knife and sliced once through Klinger's bloody, inside wrist.

Once cut, they heard movement from the backside of the fish shack. Klinger stood and tried to be silent, and using his toes, slid the three-foot-by-three-foot patch of thin carpet aside, revealing a bolt lock. "Ima undo this lock. Juuust incase." He then flipped the lock to the unlocked position and returned the carpet, and the knife.

With Lester's imminent return, Klinger rolled the sliced handcuffs back together like a ring. Eliot sliced it clean in one spot, so if he stayed calm and collected, and rested them around his wrists, it should give the illusion his wrists were still tied. He sat quietly and set the plastic handcuffs in position.

Lester stepped through the door. "You boys 'bout ready to move on?"

Silence.

Lester turned and glanced out of the shack, up at the sky. "Sun's back out, so soon as this last rain lets up, we're moving out, got it?"

Eliot removed the phone, opened it, eyeballed the screen, flipped it closed. *Why did Lester give my phone number to the people for pick-up? He has his own phone, I seen it.*

Klinger shifted in his seat, slid a wading boot over the hatch to feel for movement, then faced Eliot with his eyes bigger than a Japanese firework.

Lester moved next to the door and lit a smoke, puffed the cherry red, inhaled after tasting the right one. The smoke wheezed out while his lungs automatically exhaled—heard, "Pssssst," from behind.

22

Underneath the fish shack, I counted ten pilings that held it up, all of which strung in small strands of seagrass and cemented in tiny barnacles. I waited in silence beneath the house, listening intently, trying to place the gunman's position. The faint scuff of a boot, a shift of weight, and I concluded he was still stationed beneath the overhanging eave.

Then movement. Footsteps creaked from the one-hundred-year-old pine, but not directly above me—closer to the perimeter deck. A sudden surge of adrenaline coursed through my veins that I nearly crumbled to the skiff's deck.

Footsteps advanced toward the stern. I, and the entire skiff, were floating silently beneath the shack. If the gunman wandered to the back, he might catch the faint ripple my hull sent across the surface. If my cover blew, I'd have no choice but to defend myself.

I noticed the branch pinned in the rod holder—then the snake. I looked up inquisitively at the square, two-by-two floor hatch and wondered if I should knock softly. Then a thump, like something small had fallen to the floor.

I placed both hands on the hatch, fingertips brushing splintered wood. The world fell quiet—no voices, just the faint tremble of movement above. I held my breath. Then, on the slow exhale, it came: a soft click... then the scrape of metal sliding free. My pulse spiked. The lock. Klinger had done it. The hatch was open.

The gunman's footsteps began moving again, back toward the shack's door. He stepped through it, and I heard his voice but couldn't understand the distinctive words. He may have been speaking to Eliot, or maybe Klinger, but I couldn't tell whom.

I needed a moment to chart a plan. I picked up the branch holding the moccasin. The snake hung limp, lifeless as a wet noodle, drained to the brink of death. Without hesitation, I dipped the entire branch into the water. In an instant, the snake sprang back to life, thrashing with revived authority, its fangs working furiously to wrench free from the bark.

I inhaled while a free hand clamped onto the hatch's underside beam. When it lifted, it cracked a bit. "Here goes," I mumbled. Then I lowered it, blinked, and flung it open.

My boisterous move caused the gunman almost no alarm. In fact, the rain's clattering on the tin roof concealed me and the gunman didn't move a muscle but continued staring outside toward the sky.

Klinger's smile gleamed, and my friend became steady, shifting his weight to his toes, ready to move.

Eliot seemed docile.

I faced the gunman's direction and bordering on a scream, said, "Pssssst."

Before he could complete a full turn, I slung the branch. The snake broke free from the rind and went zipping through the air and hit the man in the chest. Bull's eye! As he raised his arms in reflex, the snake latched on, coiling up his hairless arm.

"What the—!" Lester shouted as the snake worked in the venom.

I couldn't help but watch in amazement while he shook, shuddered, and stumbled as the snake remained wound tight.

"It's you! I knew it!" He noticed my head sticking out from the hatch. "The man from the skiff!"

In a panic, he dug inside his pocket for the gun, but his hand became snagged in the slack before forcing it free. He stuffed his wide wrist back inside, all while becoming well-aware that shooting at the snake wasn't the best option. Out whipped a small razor knife, and the slashing began toward the snake's plump body, but he missed the snake, slicing open his arm. The laceration sent blood dripping to his wrist. He tossed the knife and reached again for the gun's grip.

I signaled Klinger to jump toward me, arms held out like a parent catching a playing child.

Klinger leaped forward. There was a gunshot, then another, and another. He fell through the hatch, landing hard on the deck, knocking me into the water.

Shards of ancient woodchips rained onto the skiff. I clamored against a barnacle-encrusted pylon and hoisted in from the stern. Klinger was in tight grasp of his shoulder, rolling onto his side.

I rushed to him. "Are you alright?"

He wrenched the shoulder, and then frantically patted his chest and legs in an anxious wound check. "Think so."

Eliot, crawling on his stomach, craned his head through the hatch. "Go! Get on out of here! Now!"

Klinger rolled to his feet. "Eliot!"

"Get gone now!"

I wasted no time, gripped the floor joists, and glided the boat out from under the fish shack like walking a tightrope. After seconds of sitting afloat in silence, Klinger pointed hard. "Look!"

The gunman tottered down the dock steps and boarded the Whaler. Klinger and I snapped back on task as the man undocked the small boat and feverishly yanked the engine's pull cord.

"Where is he going?" I said.

"Don't know, man!"

"What about the other guy, from the hatch? I mean Eliot."

"Yah recognized 'em, too?"

I cranked the engine. It ran strong, level idle—then stalled. I reached back and compressed the primer bulb like a maniac. "C'mon, baby," I said and cranked the starter again. The engine hesitated but snapped to life. In gear, we idled restlessly away from the fish shack.

Klinger gave me a puzzled look. "How'd ya'fix the boat?" he asked, with galvanized interest.

I smirked. "Flip."

Clear of the pilings, the gunman had traveled nearly a quarter mile, but not in the direction I had expected. Instead, he appeared to be heading north, back toward the creek, moving away from the anchored *Itinerant*.

"Hang on," I said to Klinger, hitting the throttle, and the skiff shot on plane.

Klinger asked above the engine, "Wha' yah doin'? Chasin' 'em?"

"He's got my license."

Klinger rubbed his reddened wrists. "Mine too."

"We'll get them back, trust me."

Klinger faced forward. "Don't get too close, man. He got a gun, 'member?"

I checked the hardness of the primer bulb. "Yeah, I remember. He fired a bunch of shots … so he might be out."

Klinger shouted, "Could reload…"

"He sure could."

"What 'bout Eliot?" Klinger said, glancing back at the fading fish shack. "We got'ta go back for 'em."

"We will."

"He on our side, man," Klinger said passionately. "We talked, and he don't even know much of Lester, *at all*."

Lester, I thought. To know the man's name gave meaning to the chase. "With no boat, he can't really go anywhere."

Klinger ripped off the plastic handcuff ring and tossed it to the deck. "We 'ave to get Eliot, man."

"We will."

"Shamus, I'm tellin' yah, he a good ol' boy. Jus' got roped awn into it."

Lester had now passed the creek inlet, speeding toward Turtle Bay's northern mangrove wall. He led every bit of a quarter mile, then abruptly changed course, proceeding straight for us. I gave him space, turning hard port.

Klinger stood beside me, bracing his body with the console's stability bar. "What's he doin'?" he shouted. "He's tryin' aim for us?"

"I don't think he has a clue where he's going."

"He's headin' righ'for us!" shouted Klinger in my ear. "Turn … turn!"

I stayed the course and bee-lined toward him. To stand my ground now had the potential to be a dumb mistake, but surrendering to this guy *wasn't* gonna happen, not from Shamus Pickford.

We closed in on each other, and Lester caved, banked hard, bearing east, straight for the mouth of Turtle Bay. I followed him, but the engine lost fuel pressure, and we slowed to quarter-speed.

He had now gained more than a quarter mile as his bow smacked rough chop at the mouth of the bay, almost tossing him and the crate from the boat.

"He'll get 'way, man!"

"Not if I can help it." I pumped the primer bulb and smashed the throttle down, blazing to top speed.

Klinger smacked his thigh in excitement. "I know where he goin', Shamus. The meetin' spot is Ponce."

"Ponce?" I replied, thinking he would make a stop at the *Itinerant* first. "Remember the twenty-plus-foot Stamas we saw this morning? That's their boat … it's docked right outside Cape Haze Point, off the sandbar. I'm sure that's where he's headed first, no?"

Klinger agreed and faced forward in thought, gripping the console's handle like on a roller coaster. "Since we know where he goin'," he said. "Why not head awn back 'en grab Eliot?"

"We'll get him … don't worry."

As we gained, Lester began reaching for something next to him.

Klinger shifted forward, blocking the setting sun with his hand. "What's he reachin' for?"

"Not sure."

"He tossin' fishin' rods at us!"

We watched the man, and his blood-daubed shoulder, sling two fishing rods from the boat, one at a time, landing in the Whaler's wake.

"He   trin'   to   prop   foul   us!" I watched as my skiff ran over the rods, breaking them into pieces. "They won't do any serious damage."

The man, now in my mind, reminded me of a tiny baitfish, cut and bleeding, prepped for death. His entire arm was coated in a sheen of blood, dripping into the Whaler. I then questioned our fuel situation. There couldn't be but two gallons remaining in my fuel cell, so I pulled the throttle back, sending the RPMs to four thousand, settling the skiff to a slow cruising speed.

"Look!" Klinger pointed to the mangroves outside Cape Haze Point.

I listened to his plea. Lester had changed direction, bearing westerly, portside.

"Yeah, those white caps in the harbor, on the outskirts of the bar must have spooked him really good."

Klinger blocked his face from the water praying off the hull. "He tryin' to run awn the inside, man!"

"He won't like the outcome if he does."

"Wit 'at crate on his bow, he ain't makin' it!"

"No, he's not," I said, looking at Klinger's soaked face, feeling glad to have him back. I turned and now saw the submerged tip of oyster bed dead ahead of Lester's Whaler.

"He gotta see 'at," Klinger said. "I mean … how can yah miss it?"

Lester zigged and zagged; didn't know where to go, because if he did, he'd know a "no man's friend" oyster bar ran parallel along the mangroves, and he headed straight for it. High tide or low tide, impassable—he *would* hit it.

Out on the water the smallest things become second nature, in particular logging the exact location of an oyster bar. It's the one thing that, in an instant, brands into the brains of most boaters.

Lester peeked back and saw us tailing. He gave us the finger now that he'd gained distance from us.

Klinger adamantly returned the gesture.

I watched, and it was like a slow motion film in my mind as Lester had zero warning as the engine's lower unit flung out of the water with riotous force as the skeg grounded out. His propeller produced a fine rooster tail and sprayed water like an open fire hydrant. Momentum got the best of him and tossed his body forward onto the bow. The crate flipped over onto its side. Lester faced us in shock while the spinning propeller still rotated.

As we neared the Whaler, which marooned cockeyed atop a mound of oysters, I watched Lester's movements—where his hands were—hyper-aware that if he did pull the gun and began shooting, I would be ready for him. I geared my boat to idle, setting us adrift two hundred feet away from the stranded boat.

"Wha' yah doin', man?"

"I'm not sure I want to motor any closer," I answered. "I want to see what he's going to do first."

"Did yah see 'at hard groundin'? He def' ain't goin' nowhere."

"Yeah … he hit pretty hard. Doesn't look like he was injured too bad, though."

Klinger, sturdy on the bow, shouted, "Wha' yah gonna do now, ayas'ole!"

Lester shimmied on his shoulder, onto the bow of the small boat, reached below the gunwale, stretching for something. After a frantic search, he found it and leveled up the gun.

"Duck!" I shouted. "GUN!"

Even though striking us from that distance wasn't probable, we instinctual dropped to the deck.

The snap of pulling trigger echoed to us. The gun didn't fire.

I eased up my head as Lester's index finger aggressively plucked the trigger.

"It's empty," I said.

Klinger stood, shouting random cuss words.

Lester had one choice left to escape with an empty gun and took the obvious route. On the bow, he sat up, clenched his snake-less arm to his chest, and then rolled into the water.

"See'em, man?

"Yes, I do."

"He grippin' 'is arm *tight*."

"Did that moccasin actually bite him?" I asked. "I know it hit him in the chest…"

Klinger expressed a mischievous smile. "Pre'y sure it latched righ'awn 'is arm, man." And added, "Sinkin' fangs deep in 'is flesh."

Lester waded toward the shoreline one hundred feet off, compressing above the elbow in a desperate attempt to slow the seeping blood of the laceration. He massaged the forearm, where the snake had latched on earlier.

I said, "Oh, yeah, it bit him, alright."

Klinger shouted, "Where yah gonna go, fat ayas?"

"There isn't anywhere else to go," I said. "He can only go so far into the mangroves. That's the same island the crate dropped into, just at the southern tip."

Klinger said, "Wa'le, since he ain't goin' 'enwhere soon, let's head awn over and pick up Eliot and get us outta 'ere … sound good?"

"Sounds excellent," I answered.

"I could use a beer righ' 'bout now," my friend said and reached into the cooler and cracked open a cold one. "You?"

"Definitely."

He handed me a beer, and I set the engine in gear and checked on Lester's status one last time. I was worried about my license. If he had it, and the cops caught him, I'd be linked to this mess. I glanced back one last time. Lester had reached the deep-rooted mangrove shoreline, engulfed by over-hanging branches.

****

We managed back on plane, heading toward the fish shack. On the way, Klinger and I rode in silence. The sun was low, orange, and the skies were clear and spectacular. As we closed in, a boat was docked to the pilings—Flip's.

Klinger stood ready, slung the bow rope around a bird crap-encrusted piling and knotted it to a cleat. He leaped off the boat onto the dock, took the stern line from me, and tied us off. We both made our way up the dock steps and onto the perimeter deck. The blown-out combination lock dangled from the latch. The door was pinned open, and we both stepped through it. Inside the house, Eliot was lying on the floor, while Flip knelt beside him.

Flip's eyes were wide. "He's been shot."

Klinger scuttled to Eliot's side and knelt, placing a hand to his chest. Blood painted the floor near the hatch.

"You a'right, man?" Klinger asked.

I knelt to the hatch and closed it. Droplets of blood dripped from the hatch jamb into the clear water below, dissipating like the overhead storms.

Eliot labored to breathe. "I'll be j-u-u-u-st fine."

Flip glanced up while applying firm pressure to Eliot's chest. He flashed me a look that needed no explanation—face flared white as a freshly swashed deck. "Looks like he's been hit awn in the chest and shoulder," he said, then swallowed hard. "From the back."

Klinger's deep breaths meant he also understood what had happened. His eyes widened, and he swept away some clutter surrounding Eliot. "Yah saved me," he said to Eliot.

Eliot made fast, deep breaths, struggling for air. "Nah… I didn't save you. You saved yourself. He would'a killed us both. Jesus made that clear." He coughed up blood.

I said to Eliot, "We need to take you to a hospital fast."

Flip was still applying pressure to Eliot's wounds. "Not sure we should move 'em."

I said, "It'll be much longer if we wait here for help, and my phone isn't even working right now. I think our best bet is to take him, right now … in your boat."

"I agree." Klinger shot to his feet. "Let's git."

Klinger and Flip carried Eliot from under the shoulders. Klinger struggled with the weight but managed him through the door and onto the lower dock.

With luck, my license, my knife, and Klinger's open wallet were on the floor, having fallen out when Lester tried for his gun. Before leaving, I swept for anything that might lead back to Klinger, me, or any of us. I wondered if returning to clean up the blood, wipe away our evidence would help, but realized a crime had been committed, and I should leave what I could alone after retrieving all my items.

At the water, Flip held Eliot while Klinger slung mullet like a nut job into the water.

I grew frustrated watching him waste time tossing mullet when I was confident Eliot couldn't care less if he were lying on dead fish—but said nothing. I stepped onto the lower dock.

"You're riding with him, right?" I asked a shocked, sober-faced Klinger.

"Yeah, I'm wit 'em, man."

Once enough room had been cleared, we all helped load Eliot into the boat.

I turned to my friend. "Klinger, when you motor past Cape Haze Point, try your phone signal. You might be able to call ahead and have the medics waiting at the house. Flip's place is the quickest spot to meet the paramedics from where we are."

"Here," Eliot said, struggling, reaching into his pocket. "Take this."

Eliot handed Klinger a cell phone. "Take the crate to … Ponce … when they call." He was weakening. "…and tell … my wife … I love her … please, and give my share of the money to…"

Klinger's tan face turned white as the sand on Siesta Key Beach. He took the phone from Eliot, passed it up to me.

I gripped Eliot's rugged hand. "Don't worry. I'll get it done."

Klinger motioned to stand. "Sure yah don't need a han' with the crate?"

"No, no," I said. "You go with Eliot. I'll go pick up the crate and bring it where it needs to go. We can figure things out later. Just get going. He needs help now." I paused, briefly considering that a man being shot would almost certainly trigger an immediate police investigation—best to stay quiet. "Hey, real quick," I said to all. "Say nothing to the police about the crate, cool? As of right now, we heard gunshots and ran to help. That's all, okay? We found Eliot like this."

Both Klinger and Flip understood my plea and agreed. It was no surprise none of us believed the cops should know anything about the crate, or its unknown contents.

I untied the lines from the dock cleats and pushed the Sheffield off. They had about a thirty-minute ride ahead of them, whereas I had an hour's ride.

As they pulled away, I heard Elliot say to Klinger, "It's not your fault, nope."

I stepped to the front door and its blown-out lock and wondered if I'd ever again see this place the same. The thought of it no longer filled me with joy or excitement, but in its place, anger and fear. Knowing a man had been shot in it for whatever reason was acidic to my senses.

I wasted no more time and boarded my skiff, compressed the primer bulb, and cranked the engine. I slammed the boat in gear and hauled for the Whaler.

The ride to it was bleak. Above, a small cloud was squeezing out its last remaining drops of rain. I caught a few on my tongue.

I approached the small boat using caution, in case Lester was hiding among the mangrove fringe, waiting to return and free it. But nothing had changed since I'd left it—stuck on a big ol' oyster bed. I pulled in close, anchored my boat, and waded over, which seemed to be the easiest part.

Loading the crate hadn't gone as planned. I was surprised it didn't burst open when it struck the oyster bar. But it had been built to survive a drop from a plane, and aside from a dented corner, it remained intact, and for most of the fifty-foot trek back to my skiff, the crate spent forty feet of it half-submerged.

I idled away from the oyster bed angry. Toward the west, the sun was setting, spreading its orange glow, shooting dim light beams across the resting water's surface. The storms had dissolved into ashen smudges, and when the wind turned right, I rode with it, like a wave at the beach.

23

Running on fumes, I pushed past the first channel marker leading into Ponce de Leon Inlet. During the trip, every time the engine sputtered, I nearly had a heart attack.

As I sat afloat, I pulled out Eliot's phone, flipped it open. It had multiple missed calls, all of which were from someone named Janet. His wife, I figured. After a quick tussle with the events. I gathered my thoughts, inhaled, and dialed her back.

"Hello?" the woman said on the other end.

"Hello … Janet?" I asked.

"Eliot, is that you? You sound funny."

"No, ma'am. My name is Shamus. I'm a friend of your husband."

"Oh—"

I held my breath and spoke, "Eliot's been in an accident."

"You better not be playin' one of your jokes on me … Eliot?"

"This is no joke, ma'am."

"Really?"

"Yes, I'm afraid."

"Oh my God," she said, voice shaky. "... is he okay?"

"Well, he's been shot, and as we speak, being brought to shore. They've taken him to be picked up by ambulance, ma'am."

"You said shot? I ... I don't understand. He's been out on the water all day."

"I know ... this happened on the water, ma'am."

"Oh, dear," she said, needing a moment to reflect on my words.

"I'm very sorry. I'm going to give you the address to where they're taking him, okay?"

"Okay... Okay ... let me find something to write on," she said—and began a prayer.

****

A few cars remained at Ponce de Leon Park, but nothing suspicious. Whoever they sent to collect the crate, I imagined, would do so when the coast cleared. I didn't want to spend the valuable fuel I had, so I idled out from the sailboat channel and anchored on the sandbar next to a small patch of mangroves and waited. I tried to stay undetected to avoid the bait-beseeching fishermen on the narrow concrete pier. The pier's light twinkled in a dim, ineffective manner, and cast a weak penumbra across key areas of the boat ramp.

I wondered about Eliot's condition, and if the guys had arrived back at the house, and then the hospital. It had been a long day, and what I'd like more than anything was to put this nightmare to rest and get to know a particular lady friend a little better—maybe a date, or a simple shore lunch. I decided I'd rather end this before checking Eliot's status.

During my wait time, I felt morose, serious. Whoever wanted this crate had better be damn appreciative when they get it.

Finally, the last few pier fishermen reeled up their lines and packed wads of tackle and rods. On pastel beach cruisers, a few retirees rode along, heading toward the exit. It was closing in on dusk, and near the pier, the park's attendant sat indolently in a white city vehicle, waiting for the last occupants to vacate. As soon as the park emptied, he would chain-lock the entrance gate, and the only entry was on bike or on foot. But certainly, the person(s) sent to claim the crate wouldn't get befuddled by a ten-dollar lock.

To walk from the main gate to the boat ramp and back again might be five football fields. Doesn't sound far, but when lugging two-hundred-plus pounds, it might as well be ten miles.

As the crate sat on my skiff's bow, I wanted to know what had been so important a man might die because of it. Could it be guns, or a bomb, or money, or … a cure for cancer? I decided that whatever it was, had no bearing on Eliot's fate. Even if it contained millions of dollars, I'd deliver it to where it needed to go.

An hour later, the park reached full vacancy. That's when a black shadow rolled near the entrance. A car with off headlights came to a stop adjacent to the Wildlife Rescue Center, which sat at the head of the park. I reached for the cell phone, for any missed calls, when the phone rang. The caller ID said, UNKNOWN. It had to be them.

I pressed the green button with my eyes on the car. "Hello?" I said but no answer, dead air. "What is going on?" I whispered to the ominous night air. Were they spooked because they expected Lester? Did they even know Lester? Was there a code word or secret passcode they needed?

Fearing the worst, I took things into my own hands and hung up the phone, decided to flash the running lights. "Here goes nothing," I said and flickered both bow and stern lights twice—nothing. I tried again, but this time faster—it worked. The same flicker returned from the car's headlights.

I sat for a few moments to get a reading on the car. It didn't

move, just sat still like an ill-fated, dark shadow. I'm sure they knew I couldn't just come to them. We'd have to meet and unload at the dock running along the boat ramp.

Taking the initiative, I pulled anchor, and from the bow deck, poled closer to the ramp—still no movement from the car. I signaled using the all-around white stern light. The car began a slight roll toward the dock. They were acting cautiously. I reached into my pocket, confirmed I could access my knife—unlikely though, that it would do me any good in a gunfight. At this point, you never know, and to go down this late in the game would be disastrous.

The push pole sank to fifteen feet as I poled the skiff across the channel and approached the dock. The car was a mid-80s camper-topped El Camino. I had never seen anything like it.

A throaty thrust from the engine vibrated the ground, including the dock. Dark tint blackened the El Camino's windows.

Someone placed the car in park; its idle raised. The passenger window motored down, and a silhouette developed.

I sat still in the captain's chair and became antsy. My comfort was nowhere in sight, so I didn't dock the skiff, rather floated parallel alongside the dock planks and waited for a signal or instruction. A dark outline of a head appeared. I raised my awkward hand to wave. Then a voice from inside the car carried through the silent night's air.

"Leeester?" the voice said.

"No," I answered.

In a high-pitched tone and thick Spanish accent, the voice asked, "Where Leeester?"

"He … um, he didn't make it. I have what you want—"

The window motor strained as it went up.

"Now what?" I mumbled.

The door opened.

"Here we go."

A petite man, five-foot-tall, one hundred twenty pounds soaking wet, slipped out, and began walking toward me. A glint of light flickered off a silver cross that dangled from his narrow neck, then laid flat, contrasting against his white tee-shirt.

Still acting cautious, I grasped the knife inside my pocket. My first instinct was to find out if he carried a gun, but his stature said otherwise. A weapon of any size would stick out like a third appendage, but still, I gripped the knife.

He approached the dock and eyed the wooden crate, signaled the driver, and he too stepped out and approached.

I swung the boat to the dock and tied off the bow. The two men discussed something in Spanish that I couldn't translate. They wasted no more time and arrived at the dock, and in the politest tone, asked in English, "Board?"

Shocked, I paused and nodded. "Sure."

The smaller of the two men dropped onto the bow with even footing. The large cross swung from his chest. He made for the crate, and using the straps, heaved it onto the bow. The other man had hulk, and hairless arms outlined his defined muscles. A red Polo tightened around his chest; baggy jeans crunched up slack above his white shoes. Both boarded, and both men lifted the crate and slid it onto the adjacent dock. They said nothing to themselves or me and left the boat and carried it to the rear of the El Camino. The tailgate creaked like a chalkboard when the smaller man lowered it.

Before the men finished loading the crate, the driver slipped a pry bar out from the vehicle's bed, angled it to the lid. When he levered on the bar, the crate emitted a bright orange glow, bright enough that it opened the man's face to the light, and his eyes widened first before he was forced to squint.

"How can it be?" I whispered.

It didn't take long before he reacted in satisfaction, and using the crowbar, tapped the nails back in place. He slid the crate along the well-defined grooves of the bed and closed the gate.

They walked, without an eye on me, straight for the front doors, and got in. The brake lights lit, and the car shifted into drive, lowering the idle.

"Okay. That was easy enough."

The vehicle's engine rumbled the ground as it drove three feet, but the brake lights flashed, and the El Camino came to an abrupt stop. I wielded the knife—ready for anything.

The car's window motored down, something flew out and landed on the sandy road. The car drove off, heading toward the exit, and disappeared around the corner.

I leaped out of the boat and onto the dock, and before proceeding to the item, made sure no one saw me. The night had a fresh smell of decaying organisms as the tide began to drop again. I picked up an envelope, brushed off the sand, and opened it. Hundred-dollar bills packed the inside. I wedged it down my pocket and snuck back to the boat.

*****

I arrived home late that fateful night because I had to pole my way back the last mile or so. The engine ran clean out of fuel five minutes from the entrance to my private basin. The resident dolphin was feeding on the outside flats—surfacing every two minutes for air—*poooeeesh*—alongside the skiff. We had a conversation, and it held my company on the sullen ride in. It didn't answer of course, but the moon reflected in its tiny dark eye, and it knew we were friends.

I didn't sleep that night and remained restless into the cool morning hours.

Final Chapter

A week later, back at the house, I unloaded various lengths of reclaimed wood I had bought from a classified ad—one-hundred-year-old poplar. The gentleman I had bought it off told me it was siding from an old barn he and his "Papi" had demolished. A custom doghouse for my new buddy, Scupper.

The young cur pup was curled on my doorstep when I arrived home from dropping off the crate. I couldn't help but take her in.

I pulled a long plank from the truck bed. Sara Albright helped lay it on a pair of custom sawhorses.

"Want me to hold the hook?" she asked.

"Please…"

Sara was wearing loose-fitting slacks, where bending and kneeling wouldn't be an issue. A green hat tucked hair up under it, and a few loose strands crossed her sleeveless flannel shirt.

I began to measure the wood—four-foot by one-foot. Scupper sat next to me, watching while I slid the tape measure along, using a pencil to mark the wood. This project was more for me than the pup. Following the incident, keeping my mind occupied and breathing were equal in importance.

Satisfied it measured true, I reached for the saw, but the unmistakable sound of Klinger's truck barreling up the road caught our attention—no radio this time.

Scupper also noticed the truck. "Stay," I told her. I was still nervous and not one-hundred-percent comfortable she wouldn't run off into the street, even though she had lived there for months.

Sara looked at me and knew we would have to take a raincheck on our project. The incident at the Turtle Bay stilt house, with all its haunting details, left a lasting mark. So much so, it prompted a realignment of my priorities—one of which involved my barnacle-scraping coworker.

Klinger pulled into the driveway, and I moseyed to him. He exited and we met on the walkway. I noticed his brown boots first. Klinger's black shirt tucked into his tight Wrangler jeans; rolled up-sleeves exposed sun-blonde hair—he had just returned from Eliot's funeral.

"Wha' yah buildin' now?" he asked.

I scratched Scupper's ear. "Eh … just a doghouse for ol' Scupper here."

"Finally got 'at pup to stay, huh?"

"Sure did."

"Gotcha," he replied, and eyed Sara.

"Sara's helping."

Klinger gave me a smile, a nod, a subliminal wink. He had other questions that were on his mind about Sara, now that he'd seen us together. He wanted details on this new relationship and would inquire if Sara wasn't present.

The message wasn't lost on Sara either. She stepped back, bashful. "I'll give you a call, Shamus," she said and snagged a weighty purse in the grass next to a sawhorse.

"You can stay," I said.

"I'll give you two some alone time." She stepped toward her truck.

I smiled and wanted to kiss her. "I'll call you later."

The setting sun hit Sara's flannel shirt and she blocked it using a hand. "You better, Shamus Pickford," she said, turned, and left.

Soon as her tires hit the main road, Klinger said, "Atta boy."

"Thanks."

"Very, nice." Klinger smiled.

I would explain more to him later. He understood that we would continue another time. "Sorry I missed the funeral."

"Didn't miss much."

"You know how I feel about those…"

"Yup, prolly skip your own. No worries."

Leaning toward the front door, I said, "Meet you by the skiff. I'll grab us a couple of brews."

I went through the door, skipped into the kitchen, where I opened a cooler on the floor and lifted out two ice cold beers. Unable to find a proper bottle opener, I hammered the bottle top on the laminate counter's edge. Did the same for the second, then grabbed a newspaper article. Out at the garage, Klinger was leaning against my skiff, petting Scupper. I handed him a beer.

"Boat's lookin' good," he said.

"Got her all fixed up."

"Oh, yeah?" He took a gulp of beer. "What all was wrong wit'er?"

"Nothing too major. Had to replace the fuel lines. Really, not too bad."

"Hope it didn't set yah back *too* far?"

"No, it wasn't too bad."

"Cool, cool," he said and swallowed another swig of beer.

I needed to break the tension. "How you been? Haven't seen you since … you know … that night."

His doleful tone spoke more than his actual words. "Been 'kay, I guess." He eyed the newspaper in my hand.

"I've been waiting to show you this."

"'At the newspaper?"

"Yeah, yesterdays."

"Figured Eliot's death b'in there. Been avoidin' readin' it t'be honest, until after the funeral."

I held up the paper, showed Klinger the headline: *Mysterious Death in Turtle Bay.*

Klinger looked up and showed a rare moment of focus.

I cleared my throat when I knew he was ready to listen. Summarized: "A vessel named *Itinerant* was found off Cape Haze Point and towed into Burnt Store Marina." I peeked up—continued, "According to the sheriff's patrol, the *Itinerant* was registered to a Lester

Smith of Collier County, Florida. A lengthy history of arrests, including petty theft, kidnapping, and attempted murder were also associated with his name. He had been indicted on murder charges in the mid-eighties but managed an acquittal…"

"Crazy, man."

"There's more." I continued verbatim: "After reports of a shooting were made to the police, the sheriff patrol dispatched multiple units out to the Turtle Bay fish shack. A forensic unit determined six shots had been fired, that some type of disagreement had occurred, and one man, local commercial fisherman Eliot Waldrup, had been shot in the chest and shoulder.

"It didn't take law enforcement long to find the abandoned Whaler marooned on an oyster bed at the Turtle Bay Inlet. The boat was not registered and had no identification that led back to anyone."

Klinger drank, said, "Still hard t'believe."

I peeked up to him. "My favorite part," I said, and finished the article. "It wasn't long after that a group of soaring turkey vultures caught the attention of an FWC officer. After investigating deeper, the officer found the source of the vulture's appeal: the remains of whom would later be identified as the infamous Lester Smith. His body had been stripped and eaten by wild salt hogs, leaving just a Zippo, a skull, and gun, which would later correlate to Eliot Waldrup's murder. The precarious boars even ate his clothes."

"Got wha'he deserved."

I folded the paper, stuck it down my back pocket. We both drank some beer in thought.

"How was the funeral?" I asked.

"Sad, man… so sad. Had no'idea what a religious man Eliot is. He never said anything me 'bout it."

"Well, the tolerable ones don't broadcast their faith."

Klinger zoned out in a daydream expression. I let him. He came back with, "Ended up bein' like a hun'red people. All 'is ol' friends, family. Seems he was a good ol' guy all 'round. Was especially sad seein' 'is wife. Shamus, she was a wreck."

I looked him straight in the eye. "I'm sorry to hear that."

His earnest smile accepted my sincerity.

"Did you see Flip?"

"Yeah, he was 'air." Klinger nodded and shifted his weight, leaning against the bow. "Still can't b'lieve all this happened. Ta'be quite honest with yah … still tryin' digest it all. I wanna tell his wife exac'ly what happened. I feel like we're lyin', and his wife deserves t'know the truth. Know what I mean?"

"I sure do. I've spent plenty of time thinking over every move. We can't say anything right now. Won't bring him back and won't change a thing. You know that, but maybe someday in the future."

"Yeah," he said, head down and kicking pebbles. "Me 'en Flip told the medical staff that w'heard cries comin' from the fish shack, so went to help, found Eliot, and rushed him t'shore. Gunshot wounds were obvious, man, so the medical staff had to call awn the cops."

I nodded.

The vibe was ripe for his next move. Klinger pulled out a spliff and put flame to it. "I guess we was jus' at the wrong place at the wrong time," my sad friend said, pulling fervently off the spliff, followed by a wash of beer. "If Lester weren't such a dang prick, I migh' of just been okay abidin' and never lookin' back, but he threatened m'kids, Shamus. I couldn't hold back."

I nodded.

Klinger's tone turned dark. "I swear he was gonna kill me, man. I could see it in'is eyes … no doubt 'bout it."

"I believe you one-hundred-percent, and it helps me justify my actions knowing that—really it does."

"I think I'm gonna change, man," he said. "I'm gonna try 'en do the right thing from now on—for me, the kids, and Mandy. I owe it to 'em." He drank a gulp of beer. "No more goin' out late and partyin'—gettin' messed up every weekend. Gonna tone it down." He toked extra-long off the spliff and handed it my way. I took it.

"What about the spliffs?" I said, taking a hit. "Giving it up?"

"Oh—no way. I need 'at. You crazy?" He paused, and we laughed.

He finished the beer, and I ran into the house to retrieve two more. When I returned, he spoke on the phone, but saw me and hung up.

"Mandy… she's been awfl'y nervous as of late. Don't wanna let me out of her dang *sight*."

"You didn't—"

"Don't you worry," he said. "She don't know nothin'."

I nodded with relief.

"She don't want m'goin' out fishin' for a while. Can yah believe 'at?"

"Well, it's kind of understandable, right? Don't worry too much about that. It'll pass."

"I 'ope so."

I gulped down the beer's last drop, climbed into the boat, reached into the center console, and handed a sandwich-sized brown paper bag down to Klinger.

"Here," I said.

He took the bag, high in skepticism. "What's this?" He then opened it and removed a wad of cash.

"It's the money I figured owed to Eliot. Assumed you'd want it."

"Thought those people didn't pay? Thought they jus' took the crate 'en ran off?"

"Nope, I've been waiting to see you in person before I mentioned it. I didn't even want to talk over the phone about this."

He fanned the money out like a deck of cards. "I was wonderin' 'bout this. Was so pissed Eliot was gettin' screwed out. I just figured there'd be no money."

"Well, now you've *got* the money."

With resolve, he said, "I think I know who I'm gonna give this to."

"Me too." I smiled.

"Eliot's fam'ly. They deserve it more than anyone."

"They do indeed."

"Might help his kids and college."

"No doubt."

He motioned to leave toward his truck—turned back. "Hey, how much is in 'ere anyways?"

"It's all there ... all nine thousand."

He cracked a grin, eyed my skiff. "Wha' was in the crate, anyway? Did yah get a look inside?"

"Nope, sure didn't."

Klinger had reached happiness, jollity, and smirked. In his own ways he'd overcome the incident. He climbed into his truck, drove down the driveway to the street, honked twice, and pulled away. I patted Scupper on the head and returned to my project.

The End